46TH

ALONG THE

SHORT FICTION

Along the 46ᵗʰ
SHORT FICTION

Edited by Mitchell Gauvin

Library and Archives Canada Cataloguing in Publication

Along the 46th : short fiction / editor, Mitchell Gauvin.

ISBN 978-0-9949183-0-7 (paperback)

1. Short stories, Canadian (English)--Ontario,

Northern. 2. Canadian fiction (English)--21st century.

I. Gauvin, Mitchell, 1989-, editor II. Title: Along the forty sixth.

PS8329.5.O5A46 2015   C813'.0108971313   C2015-907821-0

THE BOOK CONTAINS EXPLICIT LANGUAGE.

PUBLISHER'S NOTE:
All characters and situations in this short story anthology are fictitious and any apparent resemblance between any character and any living or dead person is entirely coincidental.

INCLUDES BIB:
ISBN 978-0-9949183-0-7

BOOK DESIGN: Fuel Multimedia

COVER ARTWORK: Danielle Daniel

PUBLISHED BY:

Latitude 46 Publishing
109 Elm Street, Suite 205
Sudbury, Ontario P3C 1T4

info@latitude46publishing.com

www.latitude46publishing.com

THE STORIES

INTRODUCTION

Mitchell Gauvin, Editor

I came to live under the 46th parallel unwillingly.

I remember having the thought. I remember being told as a young kid we were moving and having the stubbornness, the stark judgment, to declare how much I didn't care for it. For me at that age, my disavowal was no more profound than the fact I didn't like change. But that early stubbornness stayed with me, tinted the glass through which I viewed Northern Ontario.

Originally from Toronto, me, my brother, and my mother moved first to the tiny town of Warren, Ontario (the farthest contrast to a major metropolis you could fathom) and then onto Sudbury in the late-90s. I distinctly remember being in a recurrently malfunctioning golden Volkswagen Jetta driven by my mother as we passed Lansdowne Public School in the Donovan, being told it would be my new school, and thinking to myself how much I didn't like the sight of it: the number of kids, the way the building and its brash functionality loomed over the neighbourhood. Nothing looked right to me.

My relation with Sudbury has, unsurprisingly, never been one of unmediated pride, or even just plain satisfaction. It has been strained. It has been tested. It even, at one point, failed, as I joyfully ditched the region entirely when I finished high school. I started calling myself a Torontonian the minute I clapped its pavement, even though by then I had spent more time in Northern Ontario than anywhere else. Things have thawed since then. I've experienced a rejuvenated sense of honour and contentment for having lived in the region for as long as I have. I more than ever seek to delve into, rather than ignore, the way my vision of the world has been shaped by the latitude of the 46th parallel. My relation with Sudbury will always remain, in a word, rocky, and in editing this anthology I did wonder at times whether I was right for the job. Shouldn't someone who unabashedly adores the region be doing this?

Through the process of reading and editing this anthology, I realized what should have been obvious: does anyone really expect their relation with a place to be untainted, to be nothing but good hopes and positive feelings?

The short stories you're about to read do not roll out the red carpet. They will not allow you to keep hold of your clichés or to easily idealize Northern Ontario. They will compel you to confront whatever stereotypes you might have heard. They will force you to re-imagine the space in between the slag.

Often we feel a great desire for patriotism, a need (perhaps even a duty) to fly our town flag high and mighty. We want to announce how proud we are to live where we do — and rightly so sometimes. But the nature of place is far deeper. Our relation to a region can be stressed and irreconcilable, in addition to homely and comforting. A place can frustrate us, it can trap us, it can form our beliefs, determine our class, and strike deeply at something existential. At the same time, a place can also mother and father our children, be the bedrock of friendship, inform great art or root our humanity. Everyone is, after all, in some place from which they view the world. Often what's forgotten then is a place is never simple. It can refer to our home or our feeling of being. Places are places of paradox: we can experience a city as both empty and claustrophobic; we can find a region rocky and permanent at the same time as heartening and fluid.

Along the 46th is for both those who call Northern Ontario home, as well as for those who are hearing this region's voice for the first time. The 46th parallel that strikes across us might be as predictable as math can get, but our geography and the space we make with it rarely ever are. For some, imagining this region in a different way will be shocking, unsettling, maybe even vulgar. For others, it will be nostalgic. If you're like me, you might confront a sense of newness to the region you never expected. Perhaps for some, it will be all the above. Whatever experience you get from reading these short stories, it's not about legitimizing certain voices above others. The intention is rather to inspire new ones to speak. This is Latitude 46's bullhorn; the train whistle signalling a new journey; the signal from smoke rings wafting from both campfires and smokestacks. This is the opening call for all of you to answer.

We'd love to hear your voice.

STELLAR

Darlene Naponse

The lonesome room was longer than wide. A bar and four tables filled the space. She stared at the chipped, aero blue paint on the wall as He brushed past her and sat down, wrapping his legs around the barstool.

"Give this Anishnabe Kwe another wine and me another." His black hair didn't move when He sat up. "Tonight we celebrate."

"What we celebratin'?" She said.

"Just wait." He paid the bartender. His dark skin was even darker by the elbows. Dirty some would think, but she knows that's where he carries everything. She thought about the way those arms would pull her in, leaving nothing behind.

"We drink to all those fuckers and to the everlasting remnants of us," He said.

Both of them lift their arms in celebration, a custom they've borrowed, and one that makes them feel shame using, over and over again.

❋❋❋

After she told him the one joke she kept for dinner, a sonic boom cracked through the neon streets. The sound copied itself over and over, vibrating till it fell back into the earth through the split tile on the floor. A tiny ant scuttled toward the emergency exit. The bartender dropped down behind the bar, scouring as if someone entered with a shotgun. Dire incapacitation floored the bartender for seconds. He, the one sitting beside She, sipped his whiskey and looked around. An empty chair rattled and fell down, and bottles of beer rattled like a chandelier. The bartender raised his head, and then ran with his backpack out the door, leaving his tip and He and She at the bar. She saw tiny teardrops fall from the sky as she looked past Him. He watched her watching the sky fall and a shimmer reflected on her face like the moon on the open water.

Her wine was dull, the tannins young, the bouquet dampened. She leaned toward him, stretching her breasts forward, and kissed him. A fireball spit through the city and reached 400km south. Doom of the existential catastrophe encircled Him and Her.

Her silk blouse slid off her shoulder. He adjusted his pants and moved closer.

✳✳✳

His long fingers wrapped around the whiskey as his eyes lingered on the drink, and his lips were wet along their vermilion border. She wiped his lip dry with her finger, then tasted the whiskey on her fingertip. She wondered what he would do with his hands tonight? Would they pull back and forth, drink after drink, or fall fast inside her?

Scorched shops transformed to shells up and down the street. Black ash floated down the avenues like a late April snowfall, falling onto cars, hiding bikes and garbage bins. Alarms rang in the distance. The scatter of a meteor littered the city.

He and She stood outside the bar's door. The other shop owners gathered out along the sidewalk with shovels, clearing the meteorite pieces off their stretch of sidewalk. Side by side they cleaned their patch of the city street. Chunks of meteorite piled up on the street like snowbanks.

"Ugly rocks, not stardust," He said and passed her a chunk.

She examined it and then licked it. The troilite, an iron sulfide in the meteorite, tasted like forgiveness. She gave the chunk back to him. He threw it back to the city street. He watched her fingers travel through her dark hair, unsteady and caught in a knot. She pulled, tugged and freed her hands, then returned inside the bar. He poured himself a beer and her another wine. She turned quickly on her wooden stool to face the man with long fingers.

"What do you miss the most?" She said.

"I miss the smell of a fresh kill." He paused and looked at the cement wall. "And watching a storm roll in over the maples."

The night dipped, gasped, and disappeared past the dirty, glass window. The worthless stench of the city became silent. She wanted his hands to drop onto her lap, as the drops of her wine did. Just as he sat up, his worn cotton shirt untucked from his jeans. He was far from home. The concrete ate any familiarity he had with the area. Though

She was even farther from her home, she hunted in the city streets. Survival was easy for her.

He touched her arm as he stretched forward with laughter. His arm and chest fell into her, against her side. She bloomed and loosened her shoulders.

They turned and watched outside the bar. Under the neon light, a woman ran past them as a river of tears opened up and followed her. A man with a mustache shouted in worry. Dust ascended above the old buildings.

"I fucken hate neon," She said.

"It's too beautiful to love."

He went around the bar and poured them another. He grabbed a clean glass for her, then removed the head of foam off his beer. He was never a bartender, but could replicate any great action.

Standing straight at the wooden bar, she remembered she had to pee. Her swagger was slow. He watched as her skirt fell off her hip. Her flat ass cued to him he was home now. She had lipstick in her purse—she had bought it at the drugstore. She took it out of the package and puckered her lips, outlining them the same way she outlined her last painting, and then filled in the lush of her bloodline.

❊❊❊

His hands—the very ones she ached for—added money to the music box. A sad song started, and, as she exited the bathroom door, she pulled her skirt an inch higher. He yanked her hand and pulled her toward him as an earthquake erupted. She held on to him as her high heels wobbled. She looped her finger in his jeans and leaned into him. His one move since he was a teenager was to arch his back. So he did. Her hands then fell onto his ass and his cock pushed hard on her. She pulled him even closer.

Outside the bar window, men and women fought each other for a piece of the unexpected meteorite. Running, directionless, a woman fell outside the grocery store across the street from the bar. The grocer, who was staring at the sky, impulsively picked her up. They held each other while their cries echoed.

❊❊❊

In between the moments when she remembered home and laughter, she spilled wine on her open skin. He bent over and licked the wine off her breasts. A glimpse of a scar along her shoulder intrigued him. Her silk blouse covered most of it, but one part of her beaten past showed. He slowly lifted back her blouse and, as his hands moved toward the scar, she caught his hand. He looked her in the eyes, then down toward their hands. He took her hands and moved them toward his knees. He whispered into the scar. She held on to his kneecaps as if she was holding the gunwale of a boat ready to reach 90kms/hr. His hands followed the crevice of the scar.

The two drunks turned toward the brick wall as more falling meteorites shimmered. With eyes closed, the two held hands. She saw his shadow through her closed eyes and it turned to full darkness. They opened their eyes.

"Illuminated and lost."

"Do you want another?"

In front of the bar, a yellow mutt chewed on the shattered meteorite and ran away with a four-foot piece of rock shaped like a two-by-four in his mouth. Clamped to the strange stone, his teeth glowed.

The next record dropped down in the jukebox and scratched out a song. His long fingers slid under her shirt. Her heels landed in rhythm next to his, forgetting to search or fail to remember.

❋❋❋

An air blast punched through the city, flattening the surviving buildings around them. Winds ripped through concrete, glass, and steel. Luminous pieces of another world covered the road. Concrete and oiled asphalt disappeared. If this had been the years before the horizon changed, blueberries would have dried on birch and rock would have stood between the sky and earth.

He placed his hands on her, holding her closer. He and She finished their dance with a kiss and moved toward the music box. She looked, glanced up toward the bar: pattern recognition played by the best.

She felt her breasts expand with breath. Her hips fell toward him, the same hips that hid a history of evasion. She exhaled. Her hands always found the spot straight along the crease of his blue jeans.

✳✳✳

When the tsunami hit, it hollowed out the great lake and swallowed the nearby buildings. Water surged through the streets, rolling cars and floating people. The great force split the lake's floorbed open. Serpents swam again in this world. They swam in packs and floated passed the bar window.

A hundred-year-old oak drifted toward the glass window of the bar. Its branch caught between a sunken car and building rubble. The drunkard reached for the door and swam up toward the branch. He kicked the branch and it did not move. He kicked it again and it did not move. He tried to heave the branch but he only lost grip and started to float away. He dove down toward the oak and pushed its roots. The serpents swam around Him, creating a vortex, loosening the oak. The great oak floated to the surface. The serpents disappeared. He swam back into the bar.

Pushing back his long, wet hair from his face, She braided his hair as he watched the paint chip off the wall. She looked out the window and saw only under. He turned and pulled her near him. He kissed her neck. She breathed in and breathed out laughter. No real joke or reason to laugh, just a good reminder of existence. He laughed with her. He stood, soaked his fingers in his beer and touched her lips. She tasted only the roots of the oak.

Old star parts floated above the bar.

She and He had another.

Stellar was originally published in the Spring 2015 issue of the Yellow Medicine Review: A Journal of Indigenous Literature, Art, and Thought.

THE KILLER BENEATH ME

Rob Dominelli

In the Sudbury Jail, a typical range has around eight small cells where prisoners are double-bunked after lock-up, and a day area. There is a small television at the far end of the range that only the first three cells nearest to it can see after inmates are locked down for the night. These cells are usually occupied by those cons who are on the range the longest, and when a prisoner is shipped out or otherwise leaves the range for whatever reason everyone else gets to move one bunk closer to the TV.

Needless to say, this can be a joyous occasion for the occupant of the fourth cell, and in my younger years, when I got to move into the prime real estate area I would make quite a spectacle of my triumphant relocation. I'd pack my belongings in a pillowcase, do a little dance and sing the theme song from *The Jeffersons* while I strutted on down the range. *"Lawdy Lawdy, I wonda what the po' folk watchin' tonight? Lawdy, Lawdy!"* I'd cry.

The older guys got the joke, the younger ones just thought I was racist.

Generation gap I guess.

The problem with doing extended periods of time is weight gain. There is very limited movement in the SDJ, and while they feed you well, it's a lot of empty calories and junk. I always snored, but as I got heavier I got louder. Snoring, as it turns out, makes you ineligible to move toward the television. The two loudest snorers are relegated to the furthest cell from the TV. I didn't mind, after all it was only polite. People awaiting trial tended to have a hard time sleeping and the last thing they needed was a chainsaw revving up and down next to them all night. Besides, I've always been a constant reader and one thing jail had no shortage of was books.

Awaiting trial in 2005, I was double bunked with a large, longhaired and bearded guy named Dean. He had shot and killed a guy in a drug deal gone bad and was awaiting trial for second-degree murder. When I walked into his cell and unpacked my pillowcase he stood up and looked in my eyes.

"You look like a *six*," he said.

"Huh?"

"I said you look like a six," he repeated.

I stood there looking at him, not knowing quite what to say. He laughed and clapped a hand on my shoulder.

"Don't worry," he said and then lowered his voice as if he were sharing a secret. "Only fours kill eights," he murmured. "You can see it in their eyes."

I smiled at him because I couldn't think of anything else to do.

I placed my blankets on the top bunk.

Oh, fuck ...

Most folks who've never been in trouble think jail is a rough place filled with dangerous people, and in some ways they're right. Jail can be a tough place no doubt. Local lock ups like the SDJ had their fair share of scary dudes, but mostly it's not like that. It's junkies, thieves, drunk drivers, scam artists, dope dealers and winos, guys who slapped out their wives or girlfriends ... and a whole lot of people who I like to think didn't get arrested, but rather arres-cued.

What I mean by that is, folks whose addictions had gotten so bad they looked like death warmed over. They came on the range looking bone-thin with sunken in features, they shook a lot and sometimes they were so dope-sick their skin was ashen and they spent the first few weeks clinging to a toilet. It always seemed to me these guys were extremely fortunate to get arrested when they did because a few more months on the street would have almost certainly killed them. In that way most inmates weren't so different from people you meet every day. They were just normal folks who had big problems.

Every once in a while though, you get a genuine nutcase on the range. Guys who when you talk to them, you can see the headlights are on, but you're not quite sure who's driving. Normally prisoners like that didn't last. The inmates who occupied the television cells were usually the de facto leaders of the range because they were typically seasoned cons who were doing long stretches of dead time — what we called time you spent in jail before being sentenced. These were the men who had so many convictions for breach and failure to appear they didn't bother trying for bail anymore because they knew they'd be denied. When they were arrested, they just sat there until their trial date. Depending on the severity of the charges, the number of co-accused and other factors, prisoners could wait anywhere from a couple of months to a couple of years for their day in court. When a guy wasn't following the rules of the range, if he stunk, if (like my cellmate Dean) he was funny in the head, one of the guys would walk up and tell them to pack their shit. The evicted inmate had two choices. He could either gather his belongings and call for a guard to move him to another range, or he could stand and fight. Neither scenario was ideal.

If he went to another range, he better hope he had a friend because nobody wanted a guy who had just been bounced from another range onto their range. If they allowed it, other ranges would regard the one who took in the exiled prisoner "weak" and they would be looked on with scorn. Any contraband like tobacco or weed that was being circulated through the jail wouldn't be sent to a range that wasn't considered solid. Most guys who got bounced from one range usually ended up being bounced from every subsequent one until they either checked into protective custody or hid out in the hole.

If the inmate chose to fight, he'd better be tough because he'd be fighting half the range at once. It wasn't exactly fair but that was jail, man. *Suck it up, buttercup.*

My cellmate was an exception to the rule. He grew up in Sudbury, did pen time and was considered a solid and half-decent guy up until he traded his outdoor grow-op for a kilogram of crack and from what I could gather from talking to him, literally smoked himself insane.

❊❊❊

My experience was cellmates generally made lousy conversation-alists. You didn't want to get too personal because they might grow suspicious of you or, worse yet, tell you things you didn't really wanna know. You never ask an inmate if he did the crime he was accused of, because of course he didn't. Everyone in jail is innocent, even if they aren't. Some guys will tell you they were set up. The police had it in for them. Their lawyer is in league with the crown prosecutor, and they were undoubtedly having drinks with the judge *right now*, plotting new and innovative ways to fuck them over. The local newspapers made a small error while reporting their court case so, you guessed it, the reporters have it in for them as well. Those kinds of cellmates are the worst because they worry so much they can't sleep, and keep you up half the night bemoaning the unfairness of it all.

Other inmates are stone quiet, which is nice for a while, but can become disconcerting. There is a single stainless steel toilet to share after you're locked down for the night, and if I gotta piss and shit with another grown man less than two feet away, I'd like to get to know him, at least a little bit.

As a cost saving measure, inmates are locked in their respective cells from 8 p.m. to 8 a.m. every day. The television stays on until 10 or 11, depending on the mood of the guard on duty. The institution lights are left on until at least nine, so the less fortunate guys with no view can read, write or play cards with their bunk mates. This is how I got to know Dean Sellers, alleged murderer and madman.

He was a big guy with thick, muscular arms that were covered in crude jail tattoos. He was affable enough, but there was something slightly off-kilter about the way he looked at people. I'd often catch him watching the other prisoners with a small grin, like he was just about to chuckle, but he never did.

"See that guy, Bobby? He's a 5. Don't trust him. Don't gamble with him, don't tell him anything. He'll fold under questioning."

"Okay, I might regret this, but I gotta know ... what the fuck is up with the numbers, Dean?" I asked.

"Come here," he said, beckoning me toward our cell. During a typical day, our cells were shut from around 8:30 a.m. to 3:00 p.m., and then unlocked and opened until lock down in the evening so we could move freely from our bunks to the day area. I followed him to our cage.

He dug through his collection of books and pulled out an old beat-up paperback and handed it to me.

The cover was blue and illustrated with numbers and roman numerals. *The Complete Book of Numerology* by Joyce Keller. I flipped through the pages and saw Dean had circled and highlighted certain passages, even making little nonsensical equations and notes at the bottom of different pages.

My lawyers tel # 688 11777

11/77 = Good?

4's KILL 8's

88 double evil! 22 protects!

"See? It's all there man. I used to see it, the little things, but I didn't understand. Then I found this book. I was meant to have it. It's like the author wrote it for *me*."

This was the first time I wondered if asking the lieutenant to sleep in the hole at night might be a good idea. It wouldn't be the last.

✳✳✳

Once you get the routine of jail down, it becomes simple and then very quickly monotonous. Every day is the same: the walls, the bars, the smells, the food ... day after day, week in, week out. The only thing to hope for is your range gets new inmates who were smart enough to pack their assholes full of contraband before getting arrested.

Wednesdays were big days for new arrivals, because most trials and plea deals were heard on that day. You could almost guarantee we'd get two or three fresh fish come up from court, and if the Hoosegow gods were smiling on us, one of them would have a package.

It was on a Wednesday, while Dean and I were playing cribbage, a tall skinny kid with a cropped green mohawk walked into the day area.

Within a week he'd be airlifted to Sunnybrook trauma centre in Toronto.

✳✳✳

New arrivals got the second last cell, as befitting their seniority. The kid put his bedding away in his new home, stepped out into the range proper and looked around. Dean and I were sitting at the little metal table adjacent to our cell. As the kid looked at us, my bunkmate was laying out his cribbage points.

"Fifteen-two! Fifteen-four! Fifteen-six!" he exclaimed. He pointed at me, smiled and said "Six points against a six!" Then he reached for his little notepad and scribbled something down. As always, I tried to see what it was without really *looking*, in case it was *BOB IS THE SIX! KILL THE SIX!* Or something like that. Don't get me wrong, Dean was an ideal celly in many ways. He never took a shit after lock up or flushed in the middle of the night. He was clean and helped keep our little house tidy. It was the nighttime small talk that made me uneasy. He attributed everything that happened in his life to numbers, dates and years. In

1978, he was eight years old, and that was the year he got pneumonia. He handed up his notepad from the bottom bunk so I could see the weird equation he thought explained it. I'm no mathematician, but I know nonsense when I see it. I had never dealt with a clearly crazy guy accused of murder before, so I thought the safest course of action was to simply agree with him.

Yeah. Yeah, sure. I get it Dean. Wow!

"Crib?" the kid asked.

"Yup," I said

Dean stood up and looked him over. "What's your name?" he asked.

"Andy."

"Is that your full name?"

The kid paused, then laughed. "What the fuck's it matter?"

Dean looked in his eyes. Andy took a step back, and I knew why. Dean could turn the temperature down in the room with just his icy gaze.

"Anderson," the kid stammered. "Anderson Wright."

I could see Dean counting the letters of the new guy's name. He hurriedly sat back down, thumbed through his notepad and began scribbling, seeming to forget the two of us were there.

Andy looked at me curiously. I shrugged my shoulders and began counting my crib.

"You come off the street?" I asked him.

"Nah man. I'm from Thunder Bay, just coming through on the goose on my way to Penetang." *The* goose was the term we used for the prison transport bus. An inmate who was sentenced was typically assessed by prison administration and then shipped out to any number of provincial correctional facilities, depending on their security status. Non-violent offenders would be sent to low-security work camps, the violent ones ended up in places like Penetanguishene, a newer maximum security super-jail built to house inmates as cheaply as possible. A prisoner who was from the farther northern towns could expect to have two or three stopovers at different jails before reaching their destination.

"The next goose south is Monday morning," I told him.

"This shithole for four fuckin' days," he said. "Fuck me."

"Bend over," I said, smiling.

***

After supper we watched a bit of television until the lieutenant came on the range with a couple of guards to lock us all in our cells for the night. After a game of chess at the small table in our cell, which seemed to last forever (Dean was less enthusiastic about games that did not involve numbers or counting, he'd prattle on seemingly endlessly about how binary was the *language of the universe* between turns), I crawled up to the top bunk and fell asleep. It must have been early, because the television was still on.

I dreamed Dean and I were standing outside an ice hut in the middle of a vast frozen lake. It was a blizzard, and Dean was holding a shotgun and scanning the horizon with a grim expression on his face. White frost coated his mustache and beard. Just above the howling wind I could hear the new kid's voice shouting obscenities. I heard a rumble from the clouds and lightening flashed the sky. "You're a six Bobby, don't worry. I got your back," Dean called out over the noise, which seemed to be growing louder. I could still hear the skirling wind and the kid's angry voice just over the rolling crashes of thunder. I was certain something was coming, something beyond the whiteout of the heavy snowfall that was angry and determined and dangerous.

Suddenly I was awake and sitting up. The banging was coming from Andy the next cell over.

"QUIT YOUR MOTHERFUCKING SNORING!" FUUUUUUUCK!" he yelled as he pounded the thin metal wall that separated our cells.

"Hey man," I said. "Chill out, I'm up now. Sorry."

The kid grumbled and then I heard him get back onto his bunk. Dean was standing at the front of our cell in his underwear. "Hey Anderson," he said. "How old are you?"

"What's that supposed to mean?" he called back.

"It means how fucking old are you?" Dean asked again, this time more sternly.

"Eighteen," he answered.

Dean went back to his bunk. I could hear the scratching of pencil on paper. A few minutes later I heard a knock on the bottom of my bunk.

"What's up, Dean?"

In reply, he thrust his hand up beside my pillow, holding his open notepad.

ANDERSON,

12345678 letters in his name

D.O.B 1988

I didn't sleep again that night.

✳✳✳

I was staring at the ceiling of my cell when the bars were automatically buzzed open. That meant it was 8:30. The guard on duty put the coffee jug on the floor and slid it toward the bars with his foot so the spout was accessible for us to pour into our jail issued plastic mugs. All of us were given a single mug and plastic spoon in the Admitting and Discharge office. It was our responsibility to keep them clean, but years of institution coffee and tea had taken their toll, and most of the mugs were stained an ugly brown. I often took mine in the shower with me and cleaned it the best I could. The guard slid the sugar and creamer in through the flap at the front of the range. I walked over, grabbed the two containers and placed them on the crossbar above the jug. I turned around to see Andy standing in front of his house, rubbing his eyes and looking miserable.

"Ya know, we bounce guys for snoring in the T-Bay bucket."

"Is that right?" I asked.

He leered at me.

"Well, don't let fear and common sense stop you from trying," I said as I crouched down to fill up my mug.

I heard the other inmates crack their cell doors and begin shuffling toward the coffee. Kitchen staff would be along soon with the trays of cereal and cold toast. We got little packets of butter and jam with it, so the first skill you learned as an inmate was how to cut food and butter bread and toast with a long brown spoon.

I walked to the line that was forming in front of the meal slot. Andy rudely brushed past me to stand in front.

"Snorers go last," he said.

The other inmates looked at him and then to me. I laughed it off, but I was a bit wary. As a prisoner, you could let minor slights pass, but you had to be careful. If one inmate started to punk you off or pick on you, other like-minded cons might take you as a bitch, or an easy mark — then it was open season. I'd seen it happen often, and I wasn't gonna let it happen to me. When it was my turn up at the slot, I grabbed a tray for me and one for Dean. My celly was already seated at our metal table with Andy sitting across from him, where I usually sat. As I walked toward them, Dean told Andy to move.

"What the fuck for?" Andy protested.

"That's Bobby's stool."

"I don't see his name on it, man."

I put Dean's breakfast tray in front of him.

"It don't matter, Dean. Let him sit there if he wants."

I sat myself on the stool right next to Andy, to let him (and anyone else who might be watching) know he didn't intimidate me in the slightest. Now, I don't like to fight, and I've never even been a big fan of physical confrontations. To be honest, I could take a punch and had a pretty good right hand, but fighting always upset me, even if I won. Some guys have that sickness they go ape-shit with rage and want to tear a guy's head off. It just wasn't in me like that. If I could befriend a potential adversary, I'd much rather go that route, even in jail. Of course, in jail the peaceful solution is not always an option.

I finished my breakfast and placed my empty tray in the stack close to the range door. The nurse appeared at the bars with her tray of pills.

"Medication!" she called out.

This particular nurse was a tiny brunette with ample breasts and a cute face, so for many of us it was the highpoint of the day. Catcalls, or other inappropriate remarks, aimed at the nurse was an institutional offence, punishable with up to three days in the hole. That didn't stop some of the other inmates from teasing a little though, when she would call out "medication," two or three other inmates would respond with "penetration!" or "masturbation!" in a falsetto voice from the back of the range.

I walked up and nodded at her, she handed me a little paper cup with two ibuprofen in it. It had become a routine. I took two in the morning and two at night to soothe an ache I had in my right hip that had been nagging me since I broke it as a kid.

"Fucking bug-juice, huh? No wonder you fucking snore. Better not be taking that shit tonight." Andy said from behind me. By bug juice, he meant Seroquel, an anti-psychotic medication that jail doctors gave out to inmates like candy. It was prescribed to the more nervous guys to calm them down and help them sleep. Drug addicts fresh off the street often played up their mental issues to get a higher daily dose, then walked around the range like zombies all day. Old school cons didn't trust the stuff and regarded prisoners who took it as weaklings who couldn't handle doing their time. I tended to agree with that notion.

"That's pain medication," I said, "and whatever the fuck I take is none of your business."

We looked at each other for a minute in silence. The other guys were watching too.

"You just better not snore tonight," he spat, then walked back into his cell.

Whether I liked it or not, this kid was going to be a problem.

✻✻✻

The guard called out three names for court. One was Dean, the first part of his Preliminary Inquiry started this morning. As he pulled on his orange jumpsuit, I wished him luck.

"It's the 15th today," he said. I think it was the first time I ever saw him look nervous. "You know what that means."

I really didn't, but I nodded all the same and said, "Sure I do."

It was strange. Despite all his paranoid crazy talk, I was starting to like really like Dean, even though I sometimes felt like Bugs Bunny in the cartoon with the Abominable Snowman. *I'll pet him and squeeze him and love him and call him George ...*

When the guys for court left, the officer placed a push broom through the bars and rolled the yellow mop bucket onto the range. We'd sweep and mop out our houses one by one until the bucket reached the end, then one of us would do the floor of the day area. We'd usually take turns, but sometimes there would be a guy who liked to do it, so we'd just let him.

Once the trays were collected, an officer would come in and lock up all our cells for the day. After that it was more routine. *Jerry Springer* until *The Price is Right*, and then it would be lunchtime. Nobody really liked the game show except for a biker from Quebec who couldn't speak English. He thought it was extremely funny when the big ladies would rush the stage from contestants' row and Bob Barker got that look of horror on his face. After a few weeks, he began walking around repeating "It's a new car!" to us, to the guards, the nurse, to anyone who would listen. We all got a kick out of that.

Andy had removed his shirt, tied the top part of his prison oranges around his waist and was pacing the range, doing sets of push-ups at each end. By the time lunch came he had worked up quite a sweat.

I saw by the look on the other inmates faces when they grabbed their trays that lunch was bad. I guessed pigs in a blanket, or as we referred to it in jail, *cock in a sock*. I was right. I grabbed my tray and sat down. Andy sat across from me, his bare chest still dripping with perspiration. He smelled like sour sweat.

"Hey man, I'm eating at this table bro, why don't you put a shirt on?" I asked him.

Andy put his spoon down in his tray, looked at me and said "Why don't you go fuck yourself, goof?"

And there it was. Andy had forced my hand. There are some very simple rules in prison; no whistling, no reaching over another inmate's tray of food, after you use the range bathroom, clean your mess. Perhaps the most important rule though is the use of the word 'goof.' You never, ever call someone in jail a goof unless you intend to fight them. If someone calls you a goof, you have to fight that person. Do not pass Go, do not collect $200, just start swinging. If you don't other inmates will say that you "took it dry," and you'd probably have to leave the range. Sounds silly right? I don't disagree. That being said I didn't make the rules, so I leaned over the table and punched him in the mouth. The other prisoners turned from their trays and watched. "Bang him out!" someone yelled.

Andy sat there with a busted lip, looking stunned.

I stood up and walked around the table to his stool. I was extremely nervous, and more than a little upset that it had come to this. I was hoping the other inmates would think I was shaking because I was so angry.

"What, they don't teach you that in the T-Bay bucket, asshole?" I said. "You said the words, now you stand up."

The kid just sat on his stool, wide-eyed and trembling.

"Pack your shit, Andy!" someone called out from behind us. I did not want to do that. Anderson was a stupid kid, and if he checked in to protective custody now, that status would follow him forever. He'd be forced to do his time amongst the lowest of the low: pedophiles, rapists and informants. He might end up there eventually; I just didn't want to be the one who sent him.

"Look kid, you're just passing through," I said. "I'm here on a conspiracy beef, I got four other co-accused all with different lawyers who can't agree on the colour of shit, let alone a court date. Basically, you're a tourist while *I'm* here until they say otherwise. Keep your fucking mouth shut, and come Monday morning this place will be a bad memory. You understand me?"

Andy nodded. I walked to the washroom to wash my hands.

A guard came down the walkway and stopped when he saw Andy's bloody mouth.

"What happened?" he asked him.

Andy said nothing.

The guard looked around.

"What happened to this inmate?" The guard asked again, loudly so everyone could hear him.

A native guy walking by with his empty meal tray stopped, looked at Andy, then looked at the guard.

"Fuck, eh? He tripped. Is this your first day chum?"

The rest of the day passed like any other: dinner, shower, television, lock up. Dean had seemed a little more freaked out than usual, and spent the whole evening writing in his notepad. I thought about asking him how his day in court went, but decided against it. Once we were in our cells for the night, I read a couple of chapters from a novel about a secret Nazi flying saucer project developed in WWII. When the words on the page began to blur, I put it down and went to sleep.

I was awoken sometime later by Dean gently, but firmly shaking my leg.

"Bobby. Bobby wake up," he said in a low voice.

"Was I snoring?"

"No. Well yeah, but *listen*."

I could see he was more agitated than usual. I listened, and heard nothing but the guard's footsteps on the walkway doing his rounds. I was about to tell him so when I heard it myself.

Whhit-whhit, whhit-whhit, whhit-whhit.

Dean's eyes grew wide.

"What is it?" I asked him.

"Bobby. Listen. Listen for the pattern," he answered.

Oh, Jesus Christ, I thought. Then I heard it again.

Whhit-whhit-whhit, whhit-whhit-whhit.

"It sounds like scraping," I said. It was coming from Andy's cell. "What's he doing over there?"

Dean just shook his head and scribbled in his little book. He was pacing from the toilet to the bars, writing whenever the noise sounded. It continued for several minutes. When the guard came down the walkway again it stopped, only to continue after he turned the corner.

Whhit-whhit, whhit-whhit.

I hopped off my bunk and gave a short knock on the wall.

"Yo Andy, you wanna quit that? You're freaking my celly out." I felt kind of stupid complaining about noise when I was such a loud sleeper, so when I got no reply, I didn't persist. I climbed back up to my bunk and lay down.

"I dunno buddy," I told Dean. "Maybe he's jerking off over there."

"You've not listened to anything I've been telling you." Dean said. "You gotta watch for the signs. See the angles, they're *there* Bobby, you just gotta see 'em."

"Hey, uh Dean ... the crown attorney ever make you see a shrink?"

"No, but my lawyer did. Dr. Wolinski, but I wouldn't answer any of his questions."

"Why not?"

"See? This is exactly what I mean. You're not paying attention." Dean answered. The scraping noise continued.

"Wolinski," I said. "Eight letters in his name."

Dean grinned and laid a finger to the side of his nose.

"I'm going back to sleep bro." I said. "Goodnight."

Dean shook my leg a final time.

"You be careful Bobby, watch out."

Whhit-whhit, whhit-whhit.

✳✳✳

Friday morning breakfasts were my favorite. Two cold hardboiled eggs, two cold sausage wieners and a cold hash brown. Dean and I sat and ate in silence for a few minutes. Andy had taken his breakfast tray back to his cell. I supposed he was a little humiliated after what happened the day before. I asked Dean if he had court again that morning and he told me the matter was put over until Monday, then he leaned back on his stool and looked in Andy's cell.

I was about to tell him not to bother the kid when he leaned forward and resumed eating. I had been his bunkmate for a few weeks by then, so I had stopped questioning Dean about his odd little actions because by that time I learned his explanation would only puzzle me.

"You done?" He said, pointing at my empty tray.

"Yep."

He stacked his tray into mine and carried them away. I walked to the coffee jug, crouched down and refilled my cup. I heard the range door open and the meal trays being carried out, then the squeaky wheel of the mop bucket being rolled in. Dean grabbed it and pushed it to our house and began mopping the floor. I told him I'd take turns with him by the day but he insisted, saying there was a certain way he liked to do it.

After breakfast, the volume on the television was turned up, and everyone seemed to agree on channel 51, which played an hour block of rock n' roll from the late '80s and early '90s every weekday morning. That morning they played *Here I Go Again* by Whitesnake.

Andy came out of his cell and hurried toward the television.

"Yo man I love this song, turn it up," he said.

Nobody did, so he walked over, reached up and tapped the volume button himself. I saw that Dean was at the doorway of our cage with the mop. He watched Andy for a minute, then resumed cleaning the floor.

Suddenly I realized I didn't have my newspaper. I subscribed to the *Sudbury Star* every week, and when I didn't have it by the time the trays left, I knew what was happening. One of the guards was reading it. I fucking *hated* that. I figured if I was gonna pay for the paper, prisoner or not, I should read it first. I walked to the window beside the door and banged on the little window. I could see the officer on duty scanning the front page at his desk. He looked up at me, walked to the window and handed the paper through the meal slot.

"Here's your paper," he said. "Unmolested by guard eyes."

I nodded at him, grabbed it and walked away. I read the headlines, saw one looked interesting and stopped to read the story in front of my cell. I opened the paper to the second part of the article when I heard the scuff of hurried footsteps.

Somebody yelled, "Bob, heads up!"

I lowered the newspaper and saw Andy charging at me in a full-out dash. He had a scowl on his face and something in his hand. I saw Dean appear in the doorway of our cell. He had detached the heavy plastic wringer from the mop bucket. As Andy lunged at me, Dean swung it by the handle in a wild upward arc. It connected under the kid's jaw with a sickening smack. I was sprayed with blood and warm mop-water as Andy's feet flew up in front of him and his head hit the concrete floor hard. I stood there, shocked. Dean casually slid the wringer back on the bucket and placed the mop in the water, then pushed it with his foot, sending it rolling down the range. The inmates who were coming to see what happened backed away from the bucket as it sailed by, giving it a wide berth like the thing had a contagious disease.

Andy lay on the ground twitching, his jaw jutting to the left in an impossible angle and a pool of blood spreading from his head like a crimson halo.

I heard a clatter as the morning nurse came around the corner and dropped her tray when she saw the kid splayed out on the range floor. She screamed for the area officer who came running.

"You *motherfuckers*," the guard said as he surveyed the scene. "In your fucking cages, now! Shut your doors. Lock down!" He radioed for back up, buzzed our cells locked then walked on the range to make sure all our doors were secure before waving the nurse in.

I looked at Dean, who was watching her assess Anderson's condition. He had that half-grin on his face again.

"Fuck man," I said in a hushed tone. As far as I knew, none of the jail staff saw Dean do anything, so I certainly wasn't going to implicate him by shouting. "I can take care of myself, asshole. Why the fuck did you do that? You think I can't fight my own battles? Jesus *Christ*, Dean."

"Look Bobby." He said, and pointed to a spot on the floor. A few inches from the kid's trembling hand was his plastic spoon. He had filed the handle into a jagged point.

"I told you," Dean said. "He was an eight."

WOULD YOU BE MINE, COULD YOU BE MINE

Matthew Heiti

It's the silence that gets him. The door half-cocked, the hotel carpet puking its violent pattern into the room. He remembers that episode they shot with the mathematician. Rhododendrons, that's what the pattern was made of. Or was that a flower? The room stinks of something sharp and metallic.

When he left the room, the springs were shrieking on the cheap mattress, and now it's dead quiet. Dark too, only a little piss yellow spill from the street. Fred liked to work with the lights off. Didn't like the girls to see his tits were bigger'n theirs. Made them call him by his industry name: Mister.

He waits for the door to click, one hand still on the knob, before he flips the lights. They sputter in sick green fluorescence and he almost drops the pound of weed he scored off the droopy-eyed desk clerk. The sheets are off the bed, but there's a big red splotch in the middle of the bare mattress.

"Fred?"

Then he sees the second thing. Two feet poking out from underneath the bed. Pink nail polish, the glittery kind.

The squeak of a tap and he hears the water run in the washroom, door shut.

"Fred?"

He returns to the door to the hall and flips the deadbolt, hoping he hung the "do not disturb sign" out, just in case they ever clean the rooms in this dive.

"Fred?" Rapping on the bathroom door. Something like sobbing on the other side.

Trying the knob, locked. "Fred, open the fuckin' door."

"No," a weak voice from the other side says.

"I'll kick the door down, Fred, I'm serious." He looks around the room for something he can maybe ram it with. Empty bottles, Chinese food boxes, the large glass bong. His red trunk with all his touring swag in it. The teevee, one of those old heavy console sets. That might work. He picks it up. Back in his younger, ex-military days this would've been no problem. But now...

He swings it, the old one-two-three, and gives it a heave, trying to use the momentum to bring it to the door, but it hits the carpet about a foot in front of him with a sick crunch of glass and machinery.

The door to the washroom swings open. Fred's there, grey hair wild, wrapped in a bedsheet, sticky red streaking his hands, face, chest and belly. He looks like some mad god.

"Did you break the teevee, Ernie?"

"Did you kill a hooker, Fred?"

"They're going to put that on our bill."

"Did you kill the hooker?"

"We're pooched now." Fred sits down on the upended teevee.

"How much of that is your blood?"

Fred starts to shiver. He looks at Ernie and his lip starts going up and down like a trampoline.

"Not very neighbourly of you, is it Fred?" Funny, he thinks, but Fred starts to shake even harder. He's seen this before, down in the jungle muck, men going into shock. He smacks Fred hard across the face. Fred starts to cry so he smacks him again, harder. His hand almost sticking there with the blood.

"Ow, what the heck, Ernie!?!"

"Shut up."

He goes to the chair, where Fred's clothes are neatly laid out. Shoes, socks, pants, shirt, cardigan. Like the invisible man was sitting there. He grabs the cardigan and tosses it at Fred. "Put that on and stop your shivering."

Fred pulls the sweater on over the bedsheet. Red. It matches. He remembers Fred saying that his mother knit them all, and there's something so damn funny about this old fart sitting on the teevee, dressed like some Caesar, his head laurelled in blood.

"What the fudge are you laughing for, Ernie?"

But he can't stop, tears pouring down his face, breath coming in short stabs. He has to sit on the mattress or he's going to pass out. He pulls off his glasses and puts his head between his legs, trying to squeeze out the giggles, but when he looks down he sees those ten pink and glittery toes poking out from under the bed.

The laughter stops like a switch's been thrown.

He wipes his eyes and puts his glasses back on, a big red thumbprint on the right lens superimposed over Fred's big unhappy looking head.

"Ten minutes, Fred."

Fred's lip starts working again. He pulls the sheet up to cover his face and Ernie sees his balls dangling there, little grey planets, over the lip of the teevee.

"I'm gone ten minutes and you kill her." Fred makes a little noise like an animal being choked. "You killed the fuckin' hooker."

Fred pulls the sheet down just enough so that his eyes peek over it, defiant. "No."

"What d'you mean no?" He grabs the bong off the nightstand and starts packing it. "You saying she killed herself, Fred?"

"No."

"Somebody else came in and killed her and left in ten minutes, in ten fuckin' minutes, Fred?"

"No."

"Then what d'you mean no?" He lights the bowl.

Fred pulls down the sheet a little more to show his quivering lips. "She's not a hooker, Ernie."

He takes a hit off the bong. "Fuck."

Fred's always so anal. In life, not bed. Bed he bounced up and down rigid as the Pope. But he guesses Fred was right. Sure, they were gonna pay her. Something out of their earnings that night. But it's not like she was looking for it.

She'd been in the fourth or fifth row. The auditorium nearly empty. Some old high school. Bad perm, but she had a nice smile, even with the braces. She wasn't underage or anything, just crooked teeth. Stayed afterward to get some old records autographed. She loved both their shows, she said, grew up watching them. Tried to bring her little niece along, but kids these days, you know?

She didn't look at them like they were museum pieces. She got them up on stage at the bar, dancing. And she drank them both under the table.

He takes another hit off the bong. Holds it in. The glass bubble fogging over. He stares into it, like a crystal ball waiting to clear, but when it does it's just Fred sitting there.

"What are we going to do, Ernie?"

He coughs out a puff of smoke. "We?"

"Yeah."

"I didn't kill her."

"But you were here."

"No, I wasn't. I went out for ten minutes. And then you killed her."

"Stop saying that."

"It's true."

"But you don't have to say it."

"And you didn't have to do it." He takes another hit off the bong. The room hazy. Or maybe it's his head. Fred's there in front of him, taking the bong out of his hands and putting it back on the nightstand.

"We both took her out to the bar. We both brought her back here."

"We."

"So what do we do?"

"What do we do."

"Yes."

All of a sudden Fred doesn't look so silly. His face feels like it's burning up, he needs to cool off. He stumbles across the room into the washroom, and runs the tap. When he looks up into the mirror, the washroom is like a Kubrick film. Glorious and gory. "Jesus, Fred."

"Ernie."

He gets the razorblade out of the sink. Dripping red, blond hair stuck to it. Chipped where it was dropped. Useless now. "Jesus."

Fred's there in the doorway. "Lord's name, Ernie."

"Fuck the lord's name." He folds the razorblade back up and wraps it in a towel, pushes past Fred into the room. He kneels down in front of the bed, peering into the dark under there.

"She all in one piece?"

"Of course she's all in one piece, you think I'm a monster?"

"No, I think you're a Mister." This makes him giggle. A pot-smoker's giggle.

"What are we going to do, Ernie?"

He slips his hands around the feet, still warm, just holds them for a minute. Then he knocks the heels together, one-two-three. "There's no place like home. There's no place—"

"Stop that." Fred pulls him to his feet, but Ernie grabs onto Fred's makeshift skirt, pulling hard, spinning Fred like a dancer, the sheet coming off and leaving him naked, except for the cardigan. He throws the sheet on the bed, and then tosses the towel-wrapped package on top of it. Looking down at it like some kind of pattern that will resolve itself.

"Get in shower, Fred."

"But, Ernie—"

"Just get in the fuckin' shower. And clean up your mess in there." He doesn't turn to look, but in a few seconds he hears the whine of the water kicking on in the washroom.

First things first. He opens the nightstand and grabs a bottle of rye off the Gideon's. He takes a swig to clear the weed out of his head.

He goes to his red trunk. The big old thing. Bought in some junk shop in Toronto when he was making a hundred bucks a week puppeteering for that Friendly Fuckin' Giant on the CBC. Never knew he'd still be dragging it behind him like some coffin, from one city to another. Doing the same old tired shtick, wiggling his fingers over the lock like some magician, the kids shrieking, before he threw the lid open. What was inside? He never knew. Not because it was magic, but because he just couldn't remember things so good these days.

He clicks the lock and throws the lid open. Grunts as he upends it on the bed. Dinosaur, cowboy, fireman, astronaut. A bunch of patched-up old costumes he's mostly too fat for now.

He takes another swig from the bottle and tosses it on the mattress. The bong, too. All of it piled in the middle of the stained sheet. He wraps it up like one big shitty Christmas present.

He catches himself in the mirror. The plaid housecoat he brought from home, his comb-over pasted to his forehead with sweat. Got to get ready for the show.

He gets dressed. Suspenders up and bow tie on last. He takes off his glasses and cleans them, but only succeeds in smearing the blood around more. When he puts them back on, his right lens is misted with red. Half his world filled with blood.

He pulls her out by the ankles, wraps her in the housecoat so he doesn't have to look at what Fred's done. He lifts her, heavier than she looks, and lays her down in the belly of the trunk.

There's something sticking out from underneath her. He reaches down and pulls out an old videotape. Sees himself smiling up from the cardboard cover. Years younger, wrinkles lighter. A twinkle in his eye like he actually believed. Believed in the magic treehouse. Believed he would close the trunk right now, close it tight, latch it and wiggle his fingers over the lock, and when he'd open it, it'd be empty. Magicked away. And maybe he could jump in right after and just disappear too.

But the girl's still there. Pink glitter on the hem of the housecoat. He throws the videotape back in. He can't tell if the smile was even real back then. He shoves the bundle on top of her and has to sit on the trunk to get the lid to close.

The only thing left was the red circle, like a porthole, on the mattress. He picks the phone up off the cradle. He could just call the cops. Turn them both in. It'd make the papers. More than they had in years. More than he had at least. Fred had a box full of awards and medals in the trunk he liked to show off. He was always talking about the President like they were golfing buddies. He'd probably get off easy. Extradition.

He dials 0. The desk clerk who sold him the weed answers. "Yeah?"

"I need some clean sheets."

"Okay. But I ain't bringing them up."

"I spilled some wine."

"Whatever."

Click.

He flips the mattress like a blank slate, covers it up with the cheap duvet, and waits for Fred to finish washing the stink off, if he ever could. They had to be on the road in a few hours. Rolling up to some other dried up old town for a show that night. They'd grab breakfast on the road.

BLACK AS TAR

Rosanna Micelotta Battigelli

The humidity hung in the air like the limp shirts on our clothesline, thirsting for a lick of a breeze. I glanced at my brother Howard. Droplets of sweat had cut a swath through his grimy cheeks, making him look like some tribal child, despite his recent brush cut. He was two years younger than I was—eight—but he almost matched me in weight. We had been playing hide-and-seek in the back lane, waiting to be called in for lunch, and I knew we could get at least a few more rounds in while Mom finished waxing the floors, a job she always left for every second Saturday. I had counted to twenty-seven when a familiar rumble interrupted our game.

"Tar truck, Howie," I hollered, opening my eyes and scanning the lane. No sight of the kid. My gaze swept upward to the rocky outcrop rising from the end of the lane. I wondered if he had ventured up the hill to hide behind the huge slab of granite that jutted out on the other side. The slab lay bare like a tombstone, tilting its stony face toward the Big Nickel in the distance. We loved to slide down it, causing our mom no end of consternation to have to patch the thinned-out sections on the butt of our trousers. The hill was scattered with boulders in between stretches of wild grasses and weeds. If you clambered down to the other side, you would be in the back lane of Logan Avenue, and then a dash to the next street over, and around Tarini's Confectionary on Dean Street—would get you to the bottom of the Big Nickel Hill.

I didn't imagine Howie could've gone very far—I had only counted to twenty-seven, after all, and a stubby kid like him would have gravity working against him on the hill. Without a second thought, I raced to the front of our house and plunked myself down on the wooden steps. They had been tarring several roads in our Gatchell neighbourhood that summer and we always liked to watch the action. It was scorching hot that day; we were in the middle of an unusual heat wave.

The rumble was intensifying and I leaned forward, wiping the sweat off my forehead. The road gleamed as the machine flattened a thick coat of tar down one side. The dark surface gleamed like wet licorice, and the steam rising off it made it look like a mysterious swampland, damp with the elemental odours of the earth's core—a dark alchemy that both stirred and repelled the senses.

Howie appeared, huffing, his cheeks glistening like two ripe apples. He scrambled up to sit beside me. "Why didn't you wait for me, Jack?" He punched my arm and feigned a pout. I laughed. "Stop your whining or I'll tell Mom you went over to the hill. You know you're not supposed to be wandering up there by yourself."

He gave me another punch with less force than the first one, then turned his gaze to the road. Mesmerized, we watched the dark machinations of the roller. Its hiss filled our ears as it flattened the black layer of asphalt over the cracked and veined surface of the road. Workers with bright yellow hard hats and safety vests surveyed the job in progress.

When the truck rumbled off down the road, my glance skittered to the clapboard house across the road. My friend Robbie sat transfixed on his doorstep, watching the departing trucks and men. I had barely noticed him at first. He sat in between his mother's potted geraniums like a garden gnome ornament: knees up to his chin, pixy face in his hands, a glazed look and mouth half-open. "Hey, Robbie," I called, "wanna play hide-and-seek with us after lunch?"

Robbie's gaze shifted to me and my brother, and to the screen door behind him. "Uh, I'm not sure." Another glance back into the house before hopping down the steps to the edge of the road. "I have to check with my mom first. I might have to go downtown with her. She applied for a job at the bakery department at Woolworth's." He smiled crookedly. "She said I could have a chocolate milkshake or donut while she talked to somebody."

I had started walking toward him but stopped at the edge of the street, contemplating his words as I stared at the road. The tarred surface was still steaming, and I was afraid to walk across. My nose wrinkled at the sulfuric-like fumes. Facing Robbie, I could see that his ribbed undershirt was damp from sweat and stuck in places on his chest. The flaking white periphery of skin around the coral patches on the tops of his shoulders showed evidence of the summer's heat wave.

I shrugged and glanced toward his screen door. Something about Robbie's mom made me uneasy. The only time you really saw her was on Sunday morning, going to Mass at St. Anthony's Church, Robbie walking beside her with slumped shoulders. She wasn't out having coffee or tea with other ladies, or getting groceries either at Albert's Meat Market or Gatchell Meat Market. Nor was she tending her garden. Unlike most of the Italian immigrants in the neighbourhood, she had no garden.

When she and Robbie moved to our street in May—it must have been late at night, as nobody saw them or a moving truck—my mother went over with a freshly-baked lemon loaf the next afternoon to introduce herself to the new 'Eye-talian' family. Mom had stepped out for groceries in the morning and had caught sight of them outside. They were talking in the same language as some of our other neighbours.

I stood back shyly on my front steps and watched my mother knocking and waiting at their side door, her red apron still on over her paisley dress. After about ten knocks, the door opened, and all I could see was a flash of blonde hair and two slender arms reaching out for the lemon loaf. I expected my mother to disappear into their house for a while but the door promptly closed, leaving my mother staring at it for a few moments before shrugging and returning home.

It didn't take long before Robbie's mother became one of the favourite topics of conversation with my mother and her circle of friends. Sometimes I could hear them when I was playing marbles with Howie in the backyard. From the screen door that led directly into the kitchen, their voices floated toward me, speculating about the new neighbours. *Where was her husband? Did she have a husband? Why did she keep to herself? Why did she move to Sudbury? Why was it that you only saw her when it was time for Mass, and even then, she appeared a minute or two into the Mass, when all eyes were turned to the altar. And why did she never go up to receive Communion?*

The parishioners seated near her noticed her slipping out at the end of the service, as the priest genuflected and bowed before walking down the centre aisle toward the back of the church, where the parishioners could greet him before descending into the basement for coffee. She held her head up as she made her swift exit down the flight of stairs and out the door, sometimes several paces in front of her son.

My mother's Catholic friends reported she tended to wear the same outfit every Sunday: a white blouse under a black peplum blazer and a knee-length fitted skirt and black pumps. The only item of clothing that changed was the kerchief she draped over her head and tied tightly under her chin — it varied from week to week. One Sunday, it was a navy one with orange geometric designs, the next week it was black, splashed with huge red poppies, or purple with white daisies.

I looked quizzically at Robbie now. He had always been friendly, from the first time I saw him in his yard the afternoon after my mother had brought over the lemon loaf. I asked him if he wanted to come over and play with my new GI Joe and plastic soldiers. He held up a finger, disappeared into the house and reappeared moments later. He skipped across to my place and we went over to the heap of sand in my backyard. My dad had just finished laying down the slabs of concrete for our new patio. The pile of crusher dust and sand near a wild patch of grass and weeds was a perfect battle ground.

Once we introduced ourselves, Robbie didn't say much. Shrugged at some of the questions I innocently asked him, like *How old are you? Where did you live before? Are you coming to my school? Do you have any brothers or sisters?* Strangely enough, he always seemed to glance back at his house before deliberating his answer. His replies: *Ten, Windsor; I'm starting at St. Anthony's School on Monday; nope, no other brats around.*

Too bad you're not going to be in my class at Gatchell Public School, I told him after our first battle. He brushed the sand off one of the soldiers and smiled that crooked smile I got to know so well throughout our elementary and secondary school years. *I have to go to Catholic School. She wants me to grow up right, learning the Catechism, so I don't end up in Hell like the Protestants and the Jehovah's Witnesses, my soul as black as tar.*

I gulped so hard I almost swallowed my Chicklet. I spat it out; it had lost its minty flavour half-way through our first battle. Before we could start up the next attack, we heard his mother's strident voice. *Roberto! Ritorna a casa! Subito! Il pranzo é pronto.*

Robbie stood up, dropped his soldiers, brushed off his pants, and took off. "See you later," he said, without looking back at me. "It's lunchtime."

It didn't take me long to figure out Robbie's mother didn't like me, even though she allowed Robbie to come over and play. For some reason, he wasn't allowed to come inside my house. When I went to get him one day, and was about to knock on the door, I heard her speaking to Robbie in a way that sounded like her teeth were clenched. She spoke to him in Italian, and I couldn't make any sense of it except for two words: my name and 'Protestante'. I hesitated at the screen door. Robbie said something I didn't understand and then I heard her say something that sounded ugly to my ears. *Vigliacco!* And then a moment of silence before a slap. It had to have been a slap. The sound made me cringe like I did when any of my friends did a belly flop at the Copper Cliff Pool. I'm not sure if the scream that followed came from Robbie's mouth or his mother's. I bolted.

I caught my breath under the weeping willow tree in my backyard. It took a while before my heart stopped thumping like a jack-hammer. I almost wanted to cry. I felt a heaviness overcome me. Guilt, most likely, because I hadn't done anything to help Robbie. *But what could I have done*, I kept telling myself. *Rush into their house and wedge myself between them?*

And then my imagination went wild. I pictured poor Robbie slapped and whipped over and over again. *Hadn't Rico down the street mentioned his father whipped out his belt when he was angry — or drunk — and took it out on whoever was around? Rico showed a group of us his welts once, and swore he would take off when he was 16, unless he killed his father first* ... I still cringe at the memory of his purple and yellow mottled bruises...

What if Robbie's mother did the same? I started conjuring up all kinds of torturous methods she might be inflicting on poor Robbie, and then thankfully, Howie burst outside to tell me lunch was ready, and I hurried in, making sure to thank my mother for the delicious bowl of Lipton's Chicken Soup and side of hot dogs and french fries. I gave her a hug, too, and I was pleased when she beamed down at me.

Robbie said nothing about their argument when he came over after lunch. I showed him some of my new marbles so I could discreetly inspect his cheeks, and I almost said *Ahah!* out loud when I saw that one cheek was indeed, much more flushed. A glance at his arms made me sigh in relief. *No, he hadn't been whipped.*

I found myself looking for signs in the days and weeks ahead that would incite me to call the police, or at least tell my mother. She would know what to do. One day, when I was doing my homework at the kitchen table, the telephone rang. My mom picked up. My ears perked when I heard Mom gasp. Her friend Eileen was talking so loud that I could hear a lot of what she was saying. My mother practically repeated everything she said.

Are you sure? At eleven at night? She walks to the Parkland Hotel. Takes the back lanes? What? She works there? Night shift? Goes home before dawn. Got hired a week after they moved here? No way ... Really?! Black blazer and skirt?

Same pumps she wears at church, face made up like a movie star. Red, red lips. Oh my God. Is she a strip — Jack, what are you doing, listening when you should be doing your homework? Go to your room, please.

I snapped shut my arithmetic textbook and notebook and fled. In my room, I paced for a while. Had a funny feeling in the pit of my stomach. Kinda felt nauseated. *Did she leave Robbie at home alone? Did he know? Surely his mom was just a waitress. After all, she did attend Mass every Sunday ...* And then came the tawdry thoughts. Flashes of memory of the magazines Rico had shown a bunch of us after school one day, on the hill near the tombstone-like slab of rock. Women with the devil in their eyes as they stared out at you from the glossy pages, their ripe bodies teasing you behind veils and boas, their legs stretched languorously across the pages, their mouths a splash of fuchsia or fire-engine red.

I had to get out of the house. Howie was in the backyard, knee-deep in the sand pit. He was playing with my GI Joe — without my permission — but this time I didn't care. I sprinted toward the gate that led to the back lane. I unlatched it, then ran aimlessly up and down the hill. A few moments later and Howie had joined me. "Are you crazy, Jack?" he said, puffing. "You're gonna kill me."

I plopped down and started laughing hysterically. Pounded the hillside like I had just heard the joke of my life. Laughed till I cried. And I couldn't stop. I felt Howie tugging at my shirt, and saw his blurred face distended with worry. After a few more strangled sobs, I pulled myself together and wiped my eyes and face with my shirt tail.

"Don't say anything about this to anybody, you hear, Howie? I mean it." I sniffed and wiped my nose. "I'll tell you what happened someday ... "

I saw Howie nodding, his brows furrowed. I was sorry that I had scared him. "Don't worry, buddy," I ruffled his hair. "I'll be okay." I stood up. "Come on, let's play hide-and-seek. I'm counting: one, two, three ... " I only got to twenty-seven and then I heard the tar truck.

Now, facing Robbie, I pondered what he had just told me. His mother was applying for a job in the bakery department at Woolworth's. *Woolworth's.* My mother's favourite department store. *My* favourite department store. Howie and I never passed up an occasion to go shopping with my mom every second Saturday. She would always treat us to hotdogs and fries, and a chocolate milkshake or a banana cream roll. If we had been especially good that week, she would buy a box of assorted donuts for us to take home.

And now Robbie's mother was applying for a job there ... She would be wearing a crisp white uniform and a cap if she got the job, and most likely, it would be day-shift ... Robbie wouldn't have to sleep alone in the house at night.

I gulped and smiled weakly at Robbie, and hoped he couldn't tell that I knew. But then again, maybe he *didn't* know. Maybe he was already asleep when she left the house and still sleeping when she returned before dawn.

"Hey, Jack," he said, his voice wobbly with excitement. "Why don't I ask my mom if you can come with us?"

"Uh ... I don't know, Robbie. I don't think your mom — " I couldn't bring myself to say it: *would want a 'Protestante' to come along.*

"Just wait here, I'll ask. It'll be fun riding the bus together. I'll be right back."

Robbie flew into his house to ask his Mom. I waited, moving some rocks at my feet absently. After finding out about Robbie's mom, I doubted she would let me go. And Robbie's mom? Not a chance. I looked up and saw a movement at the window. Robbie's mom was looking out. Staring right at me. I could feel my face warming. The curtains in the window were lacy, and my thoughts flew to Rico's magazines...

I looked away, and then back to the rocks at my feet. Moments later, Robbie dashed out, the screen door slamming behind him. He had a jubilant smile on his face. "She said yes!" He took a tentative step on the freshly dried asphalt and walked up to me. The screen door opened and shut again, this time more gently. I looked past Robbie to his mother. *She was walking toward us.*

She was wearing a coral blouse and a leafy green skirt. Just a touch of coral lipstick. And beige, low-heeled pumps. I had never seen her up close. Her hair, naturally blonde, had a slight wave to it, and instead of a kerchief, she had a flowered headband keeping her hair in place. She was born in Northern Italy, Robbie had told me once. And he told me another time my mother's pronunciation was wrong when she told him it was nice to meet a new *Eye-talian* family the first time Robbie came over ...

She walked right up to me. I had no choice but to look up. Her eyes were blue-green, and when she said hello, the voice was gentler than I had ever imagined it could be. I blinked under her frank gaze and what looked like an apologetic smile, and I wondered if she could tell that I knew ...

"I am happy if you like to come with us," she said in her broken English.

Footsteps behind us prevented me from answering. My mom was approaching with Howie, her frown obvious to all of us. Robbie's mom took a step forward. "How you do," she nodded at my mom. "I hope you let Jack come. Howie too, if you permit." Her face broke into a smile. "I get call from Woolworth store this morning. I go for interview at four o'clock today ... If they like me, I start job on Monday."

My mom's frown relaxed, but she didn't respond. I shuffled my feet, feeling my cheeks ignite.

"I'm sorry I no come by before. I ... I ... " Robbie's mom's voice broke and I bit my lip. And held my breath. "I very sorry ... "

I glanced at my mom. Her lips were quivering. Then she smiled and took Robbie's mom by the elbow. "Come on in for a cup of tea. Or coffee. There's plenty of time before your interview." She nodded and winked at me. "And yes, the boys can go with you."

At Howie's whoop of delight, everyone laughed. I felt the knot in my gut begin to unravel, and I gave Robbie a high-five. When I turned around, my mom was already in the house, but Robbie's mom was lingering at our side door. Robbie ran to join Howie in the sand pit and I ambled toward them. When I was passing Robbie's mom, she put a hand on my shoulder. I froze. "You a good boy, Jack," she said. It came out sounding like Jeck.

I gulped. She didn't have to add, *No matter that you're a 'Protestante'.* Somehow I knew that was what she was trying to get across to me. I almost felt like a grown-up with that sudden insight. I looked up at her and her eyes were moist. I gave a quick nod and smiling again, she entered my house.

With an ear-splitting battle cry, I leapt into the sand pit.

THE BOY ON THE SWING

Casey Stranges

The screen door opened and shut in the slight breeze and Mason could hear his parents' exchange — angry little bursts from his dad, then a long, volatile chorus from his mom. His mom often sounded like she was proving something incontrovertible, or spinning a story that layered on the details and introduced characters who walked through scenes with no possible end. His dad sounded angry because things in life weren't fair.

The swing wasn't a bad place to be. Mason discovered it the morning that Pavo first showed them the house. The ropes made a deep groan with every leg pump, almost like you were inside the big tree's belly.

"Can we buy it?" Mason asked his parents.

Neither his mother or father answered him. Pavo led them up to the front door, constantly yammering and chattering while the belt on his trench coat swung and clanked off balustrades at every porch step. He jiggled the railing.

"See, people? These might have to go."

Pavo was their real estate agent and had a funny way of talking and pointing at things like the stability of the porch railing or the tuft of insulation peeking through the front window flashing. He said things like "This one's just on the market" and "it's a market for young families right now."

When Pavo visited them at their apartment, Mason was overpowered by the smell of breath mints and the way he laughed at everything his father said.

"It's an accent, Mason. He's Finnish," Mason's dad said after Pavo left.

Mason's mom wiped the spoons and saucers from the table and tossed the coffee mugs into the sink.

"He's short and walks like a pear," Mason said.

"Where did you find this guy?" Mason's mom questioned.

"Jesus, Rebecca."

"Where did you find him?" Mason asked.

In his imagination, Mason and his dad explored a forest and field covered with flat stones and spreading wildflowers — a place where you could literally uncover small people who spoke with Finnish accents.

"I know how to find a real estate agent," Mason's dad said.

"Why does he laugh all the time?" Mason asked.

"Maybe he thinks your father is funny," Mason's mom answered.

"Oh."

"Which puts his judgement into question."

"Can we go see his market?"

"Do you see anybody selling anything around here?" his mother questioned.

Mason's dad crossed his legs on the little sofa and exhaled a cloud of cigarette smoke toward the whirring ceiling fan.

Next, Mason saw himself chauffeuring his dad down an ancient lane where dark ladies beckoned from stalls and little Finnish men popped up from clay jars and said "Yaah Yaah Yaah" in different, musical tones. The oldest lady offered them an alabaster jar and when his dad touched it, a smoky blue cloud formed into Pavo's face and sang "Ring-a-Ding-Ding, it's The Boy on the Swing."

Mason laughed. Pavo was right. The market was pretty good, right now.

***

On moving day, Mason's parents allowed him to skip school so he could film the men unloading furniture from the back of the Go-Rite cube van. Like his father suggested, Mason shot lots of footage from the porch, focusing on the movers' facial expressions. Mason liked the way their heavy footsteps pounded down the metal ramp. When his mom yelled "stay out of their way!" Mason took his place on the swing. One of the movers, Frankie, who was dressed in paint-splattered jeans, saw Mason on the swing.

"Got yourself a good ride there, bud?"

Mason literally didn't have any reply, so he said "Yaah," like Pavo.

Frankie looked at him for a minute or so.

"Yaaaah Yaaaah Yaaaah Yaaaaaah," Mason said.

***

In Spring, the last pock-marked snow melted from the yard, and the brown grass grew into something golden and better. From his swing, Mason filmed freight trains in the service yard across the street. Logger cars stacked with rough shanks of pine or tightly packed cubes of wrapped lumber. Dark, mysterious gliding tankers. The trains that looked best on film were the engines that pulled pretty, painted boxcars to the Barn and shunted up against each other with a thunderous FOOM that reverberated down the tracks. Then a sharp HISSS that always made Mason jump and giggle. He especially liked the switchmen in orange vests who swaggered down the tracks carrying iron rods on their shoulders. He liked the way they yelled to each other. With his camera, Mason focused on their faces as best as he could, while they pried the rails into joint.

That morning two schoolgirls passed in front of Mason's shot. They were followed by a man walking a Golden Retriever on a long blue leash. Mason didn't mind the interruption at first, but when he thought about it later it seemed like a nuisance. The two girls turned to watch Mason film. When the shot was done and the train rumbled through the yard, Mason looked back at the open screen door.

His canvas backpack was buckled and leaning against the door. The screaming had stopped. He tried to remember if his cucumbers were lined up correctly in the Tupperware. Yes, they were. And the rice cakes in round Tupperware and Ritz crackers and butter-and-honey sandwich and two apple juice boxes and a small freezer pack to keep them cool. Nobody was coming out, so he waited.

***

On school days, Mason woke early to the sound of orange busses heaving and groaning down Morris Street. Eight, nine, sometimes ten. Down the street and back again. When the first bus screeched outside his window, Mason slipped out of his bed, tended to the bathroom, chased Ricky the Cat off the kitchen windowsill and flipped the lights on. He inspected the fridge and took what fruits and vegetables he could find in the crisper. Cucumber, half an orange and a zipped bag of cherry tomatoes. He knew where the plastic wrap was kept, and how to stretch it so you didn't slice your fingers on the jagged rail. He also knew how to wipe little swatches of sauce or peanut butter from the back of the Tupperware lids. Then, when lunch was packed away, Mason climbed the stairs and knocked on his mother's door.

"Can I wear my cargo pants today? It's warm out."

"Fine," his mom moaned.

Mason picked out a pair of underwear and socks and found his cargo pants and a clean t-shirt in the laundry basket on the floor. By that time, bus number four had already whizzed by, and the school bell would soon be ringing.

"Fourth bus, mom!" Mason's dad slept on a futon in the Business Room, with one leg draped over the side, and a rope of sheets snaking over his waist and chest. His video camera and tripod were on the floor and the Mac was on a small coffee table next to a green ceramic ashtray. He always seemed to wake up in a state of worry — "What? What? What?" was how he woke.

"Getting ready for school, Dad," Mason said.

"Got your backpack? Okay. Just keep it down," his dad replied.

When he rolled over and drifted off again, Mason tugged and pulled the sheet up around his dad's shoulders. When he backed away from the futon, trying to keep it down, Mason's backpack knocked the ashtray off the coffee table.

"Sorry, Dad, sorry," Mason said.

He found a box of Kleenex under the futon and scooped the ashes into the palm of his hand. He dumped them into the deep garbage bag in the kitchen and washed his hands. When his backpack was ready, he unstrapped it from his shoulders, laid the gear in the front hallway by the screen door, and helped his mom make coffee. He found a paper filter in the pantry and pushed two macaroni pots across the counter to make room. Then he climbed on a chair and pulled a small brown bag of Black Dog coffee from the almost-top shelf. He unwound the bag, took a deep sniff of the roasted beans.

Mason's mom, when she appeared, wore her hair long and dark over her eyes, and always questioned what he was doing. From her, Mason learned the word 'obvious.'

"Are you on the chair?"

"Obviously."

"Did you make me coffee? Is today a school day?"

"Obviously."

"You're a sharp guy."

"Mom, obviously!"

And the two would laugh, as she leaned over him, hugging and nibbling his hair.

After he returned upstairs to brush his teeth, Mason saw bus number five pass, then he remembered his homework, ran downstairs and swiped a book from the living room.

***

Mason's mom had a collection of books that overfilled the bookcase, flowed into two columns beside the fireplace. Positioned across the hardwood floor were little stacks of books that supported candles and vases, and stacks of books that held even smaller books. In his imagination, their new house rested on four great columns of heavy books. Let Pavo try to sell that one! There were thin books and heavy, linen-covered books by Poles and Jews and Polish Jews. Mason was both Polish and Jewish through his mother, and she loved to point out books that were written by the Krakow poets after the war. Mason's father was French by way of Provence and he often countered with auteurs of the cinema.

"What book is that?" she asked.

"It's for my report."

She inspected it, took a sip of coffee, and said "No."

She searched and found a book on the fireplace, a smaller one.

"That," she said, holding up the pocket-sized red book, "is a poet's name."

"I don't think the teacher's going to allow that one."

"What am I sending you for? An education."

"We're learning French."

Mason tried to read the books his mother recommended, especially by writers who had poets' names, like his mom said he should. But they were filled with words that didn't quite move like other words did, although he really liked the titles. In fact he was going to write titles when he grew up. He was sure of it.

"Are you gonna walk me to school?" Mason said.

"Go ask your father."

Mason hoisted his backpack over his shoulders and knocked on the Business Room. "I'm going now, can you walk me?"

His dad took a deep, wake-up breath and rubbed his eyes.

"Where's your mom?"

"She said to ask you."

"You can't even walk him to the corner? Jesus, Rebecca."

He rolled off the futon, wearing only boxer shorts. He pulled on a pair of skinny jeans and searched for a pair of Converse from under the futon. In the kitchen he lit a cigarette, and extinguishing the match with a brisk wave, asked-

"What's the rush to get there?"

"The Fifth Bus is already gone," Mason said.

His dad thought about this.

"So, any of the other kids even talk to you?"

"No," Mason said, "except for Brady and sometimes Gio. They liked my collection of old postcards."

"Gimme a few seconds," his dad said.

And Mason sat on the steps.

***

Mason's dad kept his own collection of things. Cameras and buckled nylon bags that contained glass lenses. Some afternoons, when Mason returned from school, Dad smoked a cigarette on the couch while telling Mason about the different effects a particular lens could make.

The first time Mason tried to pull a lens from its case, his dad sprung forward,

dropping ash onto his own lap.

"Put it back! Please!"

After that time, he waited until his dad invited him to pull the lens, or else just waited until he was asleep or the house was empty.

His dad also bought him a great birthday present — a digital camera. He brought it home after one of his long business trips.

"It's 1080 HD, Mason. No other kid is going to have one like that," he said.

Mason didn't tell the other kids about it, but they found out.

"What are you making movies about? Us?" asked Emily.

"That's cool. Do you bring it to school every day?" asked Aidan.

"You're dad actually bought it for you?" asked Noah, "can. "Can you show us?"

Even the teacher, Mme. Levesque, who was still getting used to technology in the classroom, wanted Mason to show the class.

"I'll get the television, if you want everyone to see it, Mason," she said.

Mason felt this great rush of having a secret, being proud of your secret, but being scared to reveal it to the cold, hard world.

"Okay," he said.

When Aidan finally helped Mme. Levesque with the proper plug-ins, Mason's film rolled on. There was Frankie the mover, and a stocky guy named Michel, two switchmen in the service yards, the terrific painted boxcars and the chunky caboose and busses one, two, three and four. One more time and shut the door. The words "A Mason Winston Production" rolled by and Mason smiled in front of his classmates.

"That's it? That's all there is?" Emily said.

"It's cool," Noah said.

"It's just a bunch of people doing stuff. That's lame," Emily said.

"You're lame," Aidan said.

Mme. Levesque said, "That's very creative, Mason. Would you like to put it away now?" She was worried this very expensive piece of equipment would be somehow damaged in her class, and then the emails, the phone calls, the headaches ...

"That's called an establishing shot," Mason said, when Jenna asked about all the trains.

"I still think you could have done more with it," she said.

Then Emily piped up, intending her opinion to be the final word.

"If that's all you're going to show us, then I have to say it's weird. And you're weird."

Mason fumbled with some of the straps on the camera case, then the camera slipped from his hands and landed lens-first on the floor. He picked up the lens cap and shoved the whole rig back into his backpack.

"And you're a pretentious whore!" Mason yelled, before running out.

✳✳✳

At home, on his swing, Mason showed his dad the footage.

"Cool, Mason, but you have to think more about setting up the shot. Art is all about composition."

Mason held his camera in one hand and cupped the cracked lens with his other.

He thought about many things, including composition. His mother was arguing inside again, this time with a faraway voice on the other end of a phone.

"Pierre," she said, "can you please come in here."

"Why does this always revolve around me?" Mason's dad said, to no one in particular.

From over the rooftops the school bell rang then the busses began their journey home. Mason brought the camera into focus as the busses turned out of the school yard. Six, seven, eight. Lay them straight.

From inside the house he heard his dad yell.

"Well who *is* this girl?"

A boy from class named Giovanni walked by and waved. A girl, Emmylou, younger than Gio, held her father's hand while he told a story. The story was in full-swing, but the father's eyes were focused on Mason.

Giovanni said, "That's Mason. He's in my class."

"Hello, Mason," the dad said.

"You don't know me," Mason said.

"Perhaps you're right," the dad said.

They walked on past, and at the corner the little girl looked back at the boy on the swing. Mason stuck his tongue out at her, just as his own dad was coming down the front steps.

"Mason, you want to tell me about what's going on with this Emily? Mason? Mason?"

"I'm not Mason. It's Bus. Don't call me Mason."

"Bus? That's not a name."

"Bus. Bus. Bus. Bus. Bus."

His dad backed up the stairs, and disappeared into the house.

Mason, or Bus, felt good in his swing, felt good with the little red recording light in his palm. He wouldn't ever bring that camera to class again. The lens would always have a crack down the edge, but that's okay. The camera and the cracked lens would be waiting for him when he was done the day at school. He would get home, dump his half-eaten lunch in the sink, unpack his homework, then film the busses going by from his place on the swing. His father and mother would discuss things while he shot. The final product would be a movie, a bildungsroman, a *tour de force*. It would be minimalist, abstract, even. Some logging trains, eight school busses and a family of three and only the slightest sounds of two parents arguing in the background. But you might think it was another family screaming, not his. It would be ambient noise, only ambient noise.

He could easily go back to his room and watch those movies again and again after the busses had passed.

PROMISE

Liisa Kovala

Pekka patted the small bundle of cash in his breast pocket and smiled as he surveyed the rolling fields before him, the stately pines interspersed with white birch framing the property, and the farmhouse tucked between a few towering maples. The trees were already dotted with bright green buds and the fields were ready for planting. It all belonged to his friend Erkki who was loading the remaining wood into the back of his beat-up Ford Model A. Someday Pekka would also own his own land. Sooner than later, he thought.

"All done here," Erkki said. "Thanks for helping out. Barn might even survive another winter." The last piece of timber landed with a thud on the pile. "Let's get a drink."

Pekka and Erkki had been friends since the first year they went to Wanup's one-room schoolhouse. As toe-headed boys they'd sat cramped together in the wooden desks, sharing elbow space and sometimes inkwells. In those days, Pekka spoke Finnish at home and on the playground, like most of the other school children in the small farming community. He was only four when he'd immigrated to Canada with his sister, Leena, and their parents. He barely remembered the old country.

Since Erkki inherited his family homestead two summers earlier, Pekka had spent many hours helping his friend on his property and dreaming of his own. Times were tough. Neighbours needed to take care of one another or no one had a chance. Some families could barely survive off their meagre earnings from their farms. A few had given up and moved to Sudbury to work in the mines or travelled further to work on the railroad. Pekka and his father relied on winters in the bush camp to make ends meet for the Kivi family.

"No, I'd better get going. Äiti will be expecting me to heat the sauna. Saturday, you know. Besides, I have to drop by old Mr. Saari's before I go home."

"Planning to give him all your hard earned cash?" Erkki said, exposing his gap-toothed smile and adjusting his cap against his sweaty forehead.

"As a matter of fact," Pekka said, "if I can make a deposit on his farm now, he won't be able to change his mind about selling it to me at such a great price. I'll finally have some good news for Päivi."

"What happened? She didn't like how you procured that pouch of money?" Erkki nudged the bundle in Pekka's shirt pocket. He always had a way of teasing Pekka when he was getting too serious.

Pekka frowned. "When I got back from the bush camp, I thought Päivi would be pleased." He shook his head and crushed the pebbles under his dirt covered boots.

"What does she have to complain about? She already has you tied to her apron strings and you're not even married yet." Erkki laughed. "Come on. Let me buy you a drink."

Pekka agreed. He'd been feeling so guilty about the money he'd forgotten to enjoy his accomplishments. Besides, Päivi should be happy. The small Lutheran parish meant her father could afford little to help them get started and his parents certainly couldn't contribute with his sister Leena boarding in Sudbury to finish high school, his younger siblings Saara, Laila and Timo at home, and his mother worried about a new baby on the way. He was happy to help at home, and he was a good worker, but he wanted his own place. A place to raise a family and earn his own way.

"Alright, but just one," Pekka said. "I'll visit Saari's on my way home."

Erkki grinned and slapped Pekka on the back. "Thatta boy."

✻✻✻

The boys pulled up beside the old bootlegger's barn. These days, the old man let his son Juha take care of most of the operation, but this farm had been a hub of activity in the area for as long as Pekka could remember. In the early days, it was all harmless fun. Even his parents had occasionally visited for a dance in the barn while the children played in the field and stream nearby.

Already, several old trucks and a few horse drawn wagons were haphazardly parked in the unkempt field. Lively polka music and the sounds of feet stomping on plank floors resounded through the gaps in the barn walls. The early evening sunlight filtered through the branches of the trees, creating long shadows and casting a warm glow. There was always an energetic gathering at the bootlegger's house.

It attracted all kinds: families looking for entertainment, young men purchasing liquor from Sudbury, old men gathering to gossip and share news, local drunks hoping for some handouts. Legend had it that even the former minister once missed his sermon because he'd had one too many. Those looking for more serious amusement need only enter the farmhouse where a game of poker seemed to be perpetually under way.

"Juha!" Erkki said. "Howsta *napa*?"

"Still attached." Juha shook Erkki's hand. "Pekka. Haven't seen you here in ages. Still working on getting Saari's farm?" Pekka nodded, shifting his feet back and forth. "Welcome back."

"Drinks?" Juha led them to a makeshift bar at the back of the barn. Juha motioned them to a table made of rough-hewn planks and chairs made from wooden liqueur crates tipped on their sides. "Interested in a game tonight?" he asked as he poured some whiskey into jam jars.

"Always," said Erkki. "I've got a few dollars that could use some company."

"No, thanks," said Pekka. He took a sip of the whiskey, its strong scent burning his nostrils before the liquid stung his throat. He suppressed a cough.

Juha sniggered. "Suit yourself," he said. "Wouldn't want to deprive you of your cash."

Pekka turned his attention to an old farmer trying to polka in his rubber boots around the makeshift dance floor with one of Juha's sisters. An accordion player pumped the bellows with one arm and tapped the keys with the other hand, his toes tapping up the dust in time to the melody.

Pekka tried to ignore Juha, knowing he was being bated. The two had been competitive since elementary school. When it came to cross-country skiing, Pekka usually won, but Juha sometimes claimed the prize. When they ran races, it was Pekka that had to pump his legs harder to stay at Juha's heels. Once, Juha's snide comments had resulted in a fist fight in the playground. The teacher had to pull Pekka out of the mud and sent him home with a bloody nose and permanent scar over his eyebrow.

"What do you say, Pekka? One game?" Erkki shot his whiskey back and wiped his mouth with the back of his dirty hand. "Maybe you'll get lucky. Who doesn't need a bit of extra cash these days, eh?"

Pekka absently ran a finger over the eyebrow scar before directing his attention to Juha. "Sure, I have time."

The boys followed Juha into the small kitchen, a wreath of smoke encircling the card players at the round wooden table. Empty liquor bottles littered the countertop and boxes of empties were piled in a corner on the dust-covered floor. The scent of stale whiskey hung in the air. A few bodies lay across the floor in the adjoining room, sleeping or passed out, it was hard to say.

"Deal us in boys," Juha said, scraping a chair against the plank floor.

Pekka pulled up beside Erkki, downed his whiskey and felt the weight of the money clip next to his heart as he watched the cards being dealt out to the players.

***

Hours passed. Orange streams of evening light spilled through the paned window casting long stripes across the card table. Over time the light faded to grey until it was almost too dark to see the numbers on the cards. The acrid scent of sulphur punctuated the air as Juha struck a match and lit the gas lamps, immediately transforming the room. Pekka caught a glimpse of the strange tableau of players reflected in the window's dark glass, the murky shadows exaggerating the bright light encompassing the table, the hunched figures of farmers huddled over their cards and the small pile of gleaming coins and bills in the centre. He frowned before refocusing on the cards fanned out between his fingers.

"A winning streak, eh Pekka? You've always had good luck," Juha sneered.

Pekka ignored him. It was no time to lose confidence now that he was ahead. The game continued. The drinks flowed. Every time he reached for his glass, it was magically filled. From the barn, the polka music that had filled the night air had slowed to a waltz. Eventually, it was silent.

"I'm out," Erkki said. He pushed himself back from the table and stumbled toward the door, leaning on its frame behind Pekka.

"Another," Pekka said. He studied his cards. A good hand. After this round, I'll stop, he promised himself. He watched the action around the table, scanning every face for a glimmer of hope or desperation. The problem with playing with Finns was that ever-present neutral expression: impossible to know what his opponents were thinking.

Pekka placed his cards face up on the table. Four jacks. The room swam. Cigarette smoke filled his lungs and stung his eyes. He could barely focus. The table seemed to rotate before him.

Juha paused. His deep blue eyes bore into Pekka's brain. Pekka held his breath. Juha lowered his hand, letting his cards touch the table one by one to reveal a straight flush.

Pekka hung his head, his knuckles whitening as he clutched the side of the table.

Juha pulled the winnings toward him in a dramatic flourish. "Not so lucky now," he said. "You done, old man?"

Pekka looked at Juha, but saw only the faces of those he would disappoint floating before him like rotating lamps of light. He took the last few bills from his money clip. He had to regain some of his winnings. What would he tell Päivi? How could he make his down payment to Mr. Saari? His mother would wring her hands in worry and his father would shake his head in disappointment.

"Deal me in."

***

Pekka woke to a bright white light crossing his face. He squinted. His head throbbed and his tongue felt thick. He shifted his sore body on the creaky floorboards, kicking at his boots. He must have thrown them off at some point in the night. The air was thick with old smoke and sour whiskey. Several other bodies were scattered around the room. Erkki was slumped in a rocker, his hat covering his face. One man's head was propped on his elbow, his train-like snore rattling the cards along the card table where he had finally passed out in the early morning hours.

Pulling himself from the floor, Pekka grabbed his boots and nudged Erkki. "Let's get out of here," he said. From the corner of his eye he saw movement through the open door of the bedroom. Juha was already up and dressed.

In his hands, Juha held an old hot iron like Pekka's mother used for ironing his father's Sunday shirts. In front of him, a pile of crumpled dollar bills filled a wicker basket. Pekka watched Juha pull a bill out with his thumb and forefinger, give it a shake, and smooth it over the board before flattening it with the iron. Satisfied, he placed it on a stack of crisp bills. Juha paused his ironing long enough to grin at Pekka. It was an all too familiar smile.

Pekka felt for his money clip. Empty. He swore under his breath and pulled on his boots. Dried, caked on dirt from Erkki's farm dropped from his boots and gathered on the floor. His boots crushed the dirt into the floorboards before kicking the front door open with a bang. Pekka strode away from the bootlegger's house and didn't look back.

***

Päivi looked at Pekka in disbelief. The couple faced one another on the wooden glider swing in Päivi's yard, her trim white-washed house to his left and the swelling Wanapitei River behind her. The sun filtered through her pale hair like a soft halo and the wind caught wisps of the strays, playing with them along her high cheek bones. Her cornflower blue eyes narrowed and her forehead furrowed.

Pekka looked away, past the front porch of the house, past the tire swing that hung on a tall maple where they had played as children, down to the glistening water of the river where they had swam just last summer.

"You promised! You said you would never gamble again and now you've lost it all. You've ruined everything!" Päivi clenched her fists and dug them into the boards of the swing beside her skirt.

Pekka stared at his feet. "I'm sorry." His voice was a whisper, barely audible over the sounds of pine branches swishing overhead.

"How will I explain all this to my parents? I'll never be able to trust you again."

"But it was just this once. I was winning ... and I did it for us. I promise I'll never do it again."

"You just don't get it. You're always sorry, Pekka." Päivi turned the birch bark ring he had fashioned for her around her finger. He'd sworn to replace it with a proper ring when they got married. "I just can't do this anymore." She pulled off the ring and placed it in his upturned hand before stepping off the swing.

Pekka stared at the river, his eyes trailing as far down as he could see, past the farms that lined its edge, watching the ripples travel away from him in a never ending trail, before turning down the driveway and trudging down the road.

✳✳✳

"Pekka! Come in, come in." Mr. Saari held open the screen door and shushed his barking border collie. "Coffee?"

Pekka nodded as he sat down at the large table, tucking his fingers under his thighs, his knee bobbing up and down until he realized his boot heel was tapping the floor.

"Everything's fine?" Mr. Saari asked, pouring the steaming coffee into a chipped china cup before placing it on the day's newspaper in front of Pekka.

"Yes ... well, no. I don't know how to say this," Pekka started. He cupped the coffee mug between his fingers, watching the bubbles gather at the edge of the rim. His mother used to say the more bubbles in your cup, the more money in your future. He wished that were true now.

"Just spit it out, boy." Mr. Saari sat across from Pekka, crossing his foot over his knee and leaning forward. "You in trouble?"

"No, nothing like that. I mean, yes." Pekka explained how he had lost his savings and all of his winnings from the bush camp. "I just can't pay you for the farm."

Mr. Saari stared at Pekka. He slapped his hand against the table and emitted a deep laugh. "Is that all, son? You came here so serious looking, I thought someone had died. I was prepared to hear something terrible."

Pekka was confused. This was awful. To him, at least. To Päivi.

"First of all, don't you worry about this farm. It's yours. You can work here to make some payments until I move to Sudbury to be with those needy daughters of mine. Then, you can set aside some of the money you earn, when the farm starts making money that is, and make payments to me until it's paid off. Listen, I just want you to have the damn place. I know you love it and my daughters and their husbands certainly don't care about it. Besides, I know a thing or two about gambling. Best stay away from that or you might get in worse trouble next time."

Pekka's shoulders relaxed and he let out a sigh of relief. He hadn't even realized he'd been holding his breath.

"And Päivi? Well, that one knows her mind. You'd be lucky to have her, of course, but you're young. If it's meant to be, it will happen. You're what? Twenty? Plenty of time for a wife and family. In the meantime, this farm will be here for you, ready for a bride when that day comes."

Pekka nodded, his eyes brimming. He didn't believe in crying, but he couldn't help a tear from escaping and trailing down his cheek. "I don't know what to say," he said, his voice catching as he turned his tear-stained face away.

"No need, boy." Mr. Saari patted Pekka on the shoulders. "No need."

✳✳✳

Several months passed. Spring warmed to summer and summer cooled to fall. Pekka filled his days helping his parents and working at Saari's farm. It felt like his place now. He avoided going anywhere he might see Päivi, but he'd heard rumours that she might be seeing someone else, may even be engaged. He didn't ask any questions. He didn't want to know.

One afternoon, he stopped at the Wanup General Store for supplies on his way home. The small store was lined with farming materials, some dry food items and a few personal items. A bell rang behind him as the side door opened. Erkki walked in and saw Pekka, hesitating before moving in his direction.

"Long time no see," Erkki said, offering his hand. Pekka grasped the outstretched hand. A moment of silence filled the space between them. "I haven't seen you around for so long. Since the game, I think."

"Yeah, I was wondering where you've been."

Erkki looked embarrassed. "Listen, I just want to tell you how sorry I am. I had no idea Juha was going to strip you of all of your savings. I feel terrible about what happened."

"Why would you feel bad?" Pekka stared at his friend. Juha looked away.

Erkki's face reddened. "It's just... I was in debt and I owed Juha a bundle."

"Why didn't you tell me?"

"When he heard you came back from the bush with so much cash, he said he'd forgive my debt as long as I got you to the game."

"What do you mean?"

"I didn't think he would take it all. Besides, I actually thought you had a chance. I didn't know he was going to cheat you out of everything."

Pekka's head swam. It had been a set-up. Worse, his best friend was involved. He had lost everything. His fiancée. His money. He'd almost lost the land. And now, his best friend had betrayed him. He didn't have anything else to lose.

"I never meant for this to happen. I was desperate. I was ashamed to tell you I was going to lose my family farm," Erkki said.

Pekka let out a long breath. "I understand," Pekka said. "Everyone makes foolish mistakes. But you need to know, it's not about the money."

Pekka didn't wait for a response. He closed the door behind him, the bell jangling gently against the door jam. He pulled his jacket collar up as the autumn breeze whipped against his face. Despite the cool air, he lifted his face to feel the warm beams of the mid-afternoon sun against his skin, closing his eyes briefly to see the bright red and orange dance behind his eyelids. Dried leaves crunched under his boots, encrusted by the soil of his farm, and the woody scent of pine and fir trees whirled around him. He imagined he could smell snow in the air.

Somehow he felt lighter, as though the wind had swept away his troubles like it scattered the autumn leaves. He walked down the winding road, tucking his hands into his pockets, enjoying the sound of the gravel underfoot. Before long he would be on his way to the bush camp for a few months of hard work while his new farm waited for him under a blanket of fresh snow until spring arrived. He smiled.

GRASSROOTS

Thomas Leduc

The passenger's seat of the hatchback was pushed forward to its limit. This was done so the baby's booster-seat could fit properly, but it left Dan with his long scrawny legs pressed hard against the dash and his head only inches from the ceiling. He felt as if he was being squeezed out the sunroof by his wife and child. He wanted to kick out the dash, tare the door off the hinges, stretch out and free himself, but he knew this was impossible. He was a father now. A husband. And regardless how tight the noose felt around his neck, he had to find a way to breath, and to survive.

It was mid-afternoon when the rain started. Daniel sat crammed in the passenger seat of his car and stared out the window. His wife, Nicole, drove and complained about the last two women they'd interviewed. Who would have thought finding a daycare for their son would be so difficult? How could so many people have such a different definition of childcare? Things were truly beginning to look scary, like one of them might have to quit their job. He ran his fingers through his dark hair, shuddered at the thought of one less paycheck, at the thought of being a stay-at-home dad. He brought in less income than his wife, so it would only be logical that he would quit his job and stay home, while she continued working.

"Did you see her stomach?" Nicole asked. "I couldn't help but stare. It hung like bread dough past her shirt. I'm sure I counted at least forty-seven black moles. It was like staring at some kind of skin universe."

Dan laughed. "They were beauty marks, couldn't you tell?"

She gagged. "If they were beauty marks, how come I'm not covered in them?"

"Good one," Dan said.

"Seriously," Nicole continued. "She had three dogs. I could hardly take a breath without getting a mouthful of hair. She walked with a cane for Christ's sake. How could she possibly take care of toddlers, let alone a baby?" Nicole sped the wipers up then threw her hand in the air and slammed it back down on the steering wheel. "And the woman before her. She let her teenage son take the kids alone for a walk in the forest. Like that isn't the creepiest thing I ever heard. Who would be Ok with this?"

"Don't worry, we'll find someone," Dan said.

As his wife continued to rant, he tried not to drown in despair and instead stay focused on the positive. He cast his eyes around the car and looked for something to distract himself. He settled on the gray blanket thrown over the driver's seat to hide the cracked leather. The blanket was torn in two places, so he stuck his finger in one of the holes and played with the tear.

"Leave it alone," Nicole warned.

Dan pulled his hand away as if he had just touched a hot burner on the stove. His wife was sounding more like a mother every day. He kicked at the coffee cups at his feet and their sudden displacement left a mysterious cool breeze on his leg. He listened to the hum of the heater, which was louder than the motor, then stared at the crack in the windshield. He followed the crack to the other side of the car, where his wife was still ranting on about everything. Focusing on the positive was going to be more difficult than he had anticipated.

In the backseat his son was passed out in his booster seat, his little hands clinging to a stuffed fish. The little guy was completely oblivious to all of the chaos and stress Dan and his wife were feeling. Dan smiled and stared in amazement at what the two of them had created.

"The next place will be better," he said. "Brent and Erin highly recommended it. It's the daycare they use for Kaylie."

Nicole gave a deep sigh and a bit of a smirk. "I sure hope so."

Inside their little car everything seemed to fit Nicole's tiny frame, but as Dan looked at his wife something was different. When they went to buy a used car, they argued about whether to buy a truck or a car. Dan wanted a truck, so he could stretch out, take it fishing, feel in control on the road, but the gas mileage in a truck didn't suit their budget, so Nicole got the car she wanted.

He watched as she sat in the driver's seat. Her short black hair would whip from side to side whenever she turned her head and checked for traffic. She kept her sharp, freckled nose turned up at the road in front of her, and her thin lips puckered and pressed hard together. She was bent forward in her seat, her breasts almost touched the steering wheel, which she gripped tight in her hands. She looked like she was navigating a ship through a storm, not like she was sitting in a car that was bought with her in mind.

When they were young and first met, she would drive barefoot with the radio blasting. Now, Dan's not even allowed to turn the radio on because the music is too distracting for her. It seemed that overnight everything had changed. One minute, free time spilled out of their pockets, and the next minute, it was nowhere to be found. Time was no longer on their side; it was a heavy weight that anchored them to the calendar. Their days raced by to the ticking of a clock.

He noticed when she drove she had one eye on the road and one on the dashboard clock. He wondered, if the pulse of passing time beat in the back of her mind, if it disrupted her day woke her from her sleep, as it did his. They seemed to be tangled in their newborn's bed of roots, struggling between yesterday and today. They were like two little birds obsessed with their nest. He wanted to reach over, untangle her anxiety, the knots in her shoulders, but he knew he was just as matted as she was and there was nothing he could do about it.

Restless in his seat, he shifted about and tried to get comfortable but there was no comfortable position to be found. Instead, he stared out the window and listened as his wife offered her apologies for the state of the car.

"You don't have to apologize," he said. "The car belongs to the both of us. We're both responsible for its state. I'll try and clean it tomorrow."

She threw her head back and lifted her eyebrows at his response, as if the idea of everything being both their responsibility had never occurred to her.

Dan turned his attention to the backseat where his son was still fast asleep and it occurred to him that youth and time were precious commodities and any kid stuff for him or his wife would now come with a dark shadow of responsibility. No more puddle jumping Saturdays, you could get sick, no more scabbed knees and broken bikes, these would be theirs to fix. No more red-rover, red-rover evenings with friends, only the hide and go seek of parenthood. He pushed his knees against the dash and tried to sit up, but it was no use, so he turned and focused on the rain again.

"This is a nice neighbourhood. It reminds me of where your parents live," he said.

The words sliced the silence in the car like the lightning in the sky ahead of them. It jolted them out of their hypnotized state.

"No, not really. I grew up in Hanmer — my neighbourhood looked nothing like this," she said.

"Maybe not back then, but now I think it looks the same as this one."

Nicole paused for a second to the think about it. "I guess, a little bit with all the tress."

"It's nothing like Whitson Gardens, where I grew up. Man that place was a zoo," Dan shook his head as memories came flooding in one after another.

"Every morning seven buses would pull into a three-block radius and fill to standing room only. My neighbourhood was a three-ring circus of row houses. Each one stuck together with bubble gum and stuffed with bunk-beds and microwaves. All of them with a wood paneled station-wagon parked in the driveway." Dan closed his eyes. He could see his backyard, hear the gate clank shut in his head.

He began to tell her of the times he spent dancing on picnic tables to *Grease* songs and splashing through puddles in the laneway. How he built cabins in the forest on the other side of the street. How there were trails that circled the whole subdivision like the tangled hair of a six-year-old girl and he would race through them on his bike. How he would slow time down and somersault off an eight-foot fence into a pile of freshly fallen snow without a care in the world. He told her how the Whitson River separated them from their little town of Chelmsford and how that gave him total freedom to roam the streets.

At that moment he started to say his old address aloud, grinning like a kid showing off to his parents. They both started to laugh. Dan peeked into the back seat to see if their sudden burst of laughter had awaken their son, but his little body still laid there all slumped over and still. If the thunder didn't wake him why should the laughter?

"Yes, yes I heard all this before." she said. "You lived in Disneyland," she was now leaning back in her seat, her hands relaxed and low on the wheel.

"It wasn't all picnics and rainbows," he said. "We always had new neighbours and you never knew what kind of drama was going to move in with them."

He began to tell her about a time when these two girls, maybe 12 and 16, rang his doorbell late one night. When his dad answered the door the girls were standing there, all pigtails and pajamas, the older one with a shotgun in her hands. They begged to come in. The older one said, if she hadn't taken the gun and left, her mother would have shot her father. Dan revealed to his wife how that was the first time he had seen a gun. The vision of a young girl in a white nightgown and a shotgun pressed against her still haunted him. It was something he hadn't thought about in a longtime. When he spoke of growing up, he only ever mentioned the fun he had, the good times, but now that the floodgates were open, memories were rushing in.

He told her about the time his babysitter stole food from their freezer to bring home and how she would torment their cat. One day she showed up at his house with the police and asked if his dad would help her. He said he never knew at the time what it was all about, but years later he discovered the girl's dad was in prison for child abuse.

"You never told me any of this before," she said.

"I know," he said. "It's not something I like to think about. I don't know why it's coming up now."

"Is there anything else?"

Dan looked over at his wife, she was looking right back at him. He shrugged his shoulders, turned back to the rain outside and began to tell her about the time he woke up and found his street swarmed with cop cars because the man who lived across from them had hung himself. His son had found him hanging from the rafters through the attic door. He told how the boy told him it was because of money problems.

Dan was quiet for a moment. He remembered how his parents never fought a lot but when they did fight, it was always about money and the memory of his neighbour brought back some old fears.

"What's living in the Gardens without some weeds? That's what my mom would say."

As for weeds, he told her about the sandbox kings and mud-cake queens who pushed him around, the bullies of the neighbourhood.

"As long as you weren't caught alone," he said. "You were safe."

Dan turned away from the window and back at his wife. "I spent most of my days standing around laughing, playing games and fighting with the French kids."

"You fought with the French kids?" Nicole asked. "I was a French kid. Why would you fight with the French kids? Who are you?"

Dan laughed. "I don't know? I only fought with them when I was kid. When I was a teenager, I tried to date the girls, but their brothers wouldn't let them go out with me because of those battles on the playground."

Nicole shook her head, then tapped the steering wheel and pointed outside.

"We're looking for number 136, it will be on your side," she said in her new mother's tone. Dan gripped the arm rest and squeezed as hard as he could.

Inside the daycare was clean and well organized, modern toys were tucked away on multi coloured plastic shelves like low hanging fruit for the kids to pick. On the wall above hung a license and credentials along with clearly labeled emergency exits. Dan tapped his feet on the carpet until Nicole had to put her hand on his knee, so he would stop. He noticed a picture of their friend's daughter Kaylie and he pointed the picture out to Nicole. She smiled and nodded but never looked at the photo.

The two women, a mother and daughter team, sat side-by-side with their legs crossed. They had straight blond hair and blue eyes, and they reeked of perfume. Even their clothes complimented each other. Dan watched as their lip gloss caught the light and sparkled. He waited for one of them to acknowledge him, ask him a question, but it never happened. They directed all their questions to Nicole, so Dan looked down at his son who was now awake and decided to spend the hour playing with him.

Outside the home daycare, Dan squeezed himself into the driver's seat and even with the seat pushed all the way back there still there wasn't enough room for him to be comfortable. He glanced up and down the street; every driveway was decorated in lock-stone, every yard ornamented by maple trees, and a perfectly manicured lawn. The street could have been on the cover of *Better Homes and Gardens*.

"I hope we can have something like this someday," he said.

"If you want all this you're going to have to get a better job." The words slipped out of her mouth before she could think them through.

Dan's eyes narrowed, and he clenched his fist. "I know you're a big time nurse and I'm just a construction worker, but I didn't have all the opportunities you did. Driving a backhoe is a good job and there's lots of room to move up in this company. The money will come."

"I know, I know," she said and kicked the garbage at her feet then stuffed the diaper bag in the empty space.

They sat there staring at the windshield, watching the rain drops connect, dribble down and stop at the crack. It had been a long day driving around, pulling bags of baby stuff in and out of the car, and faking politeness to strangers. The only one of them with any energy left to say anything was the baby, now wide-awake and babbling away to his stuffed fish. Dan closed his eyes, listened to his son and unclenched his fist.

In his head he went through the route home and searched for a coffee shop to stop at, but there wasn't one he could think of. He took a deep breath and started the car. The wipers took off, back and forth, back and forth wiping the rain. They struggled to clear his view forward. He stared until Nicole snapped him out of it.

His wife was sitting sideways in her seat and looking back at their son. Her short black hair was wet and stuck to her pale white face. She was beautiful. He put the car in drive and pulled out onto the road.

"CAR!" Nicole screamed.

Dan slammed on the brakes and the two of them jolted forward in their seats. The other driver hit his horn and swung around them, missing the front of their car by inches.

"What the hell is wrong with you? We almost got hit. You have to pay attention. You could have killed us. What the hell are you thinking?" Nicole screamed. "I wasn't even looking that way and I saw him, for Christ's sake."

Dan sat there, his heart pounding, his hands gripped tight to the steering wheel.

"Sorry, I didn't see him there."

"Do you want me to drive?"

Dan cringed and rolled his eyes, then removed his foot from the brake.

"No. I'll be fine," he said.

After several minutes of silence he decided to ask her what she thought of the last interview.

"They were alright," she said.

"Was it just me or did something not feel right? I couldn't put my finger on it but I didn't feel comfortable there."

Nicole was leaning into the backseat and was teasing their son with his stuffed fish. She never took her eyes off the baby, never missed a beat.

"It was because they weren't French," she said, as if it was the most obvious thing in the room throughout the whole interview.

"What the hell do you mean it's because they're not French? What does that have to do with anything?"

She handed the baby back his fish then sat back up in her seat and looked right at him.

"You're French," she said. "Your dad's French, you grew up in a French house with French traditions. You don't speak the language, but you were brought up in the culture. I don't understand why you would have fought with the French kids. You were one of them."

She raised her arms and pulled back her hair from her face and smiled.

"It's also the reason why you got along with my family. Why you married me. I was the first French girl you ever dated."

She went back to playing with the baby like nothing ever happened but her words hit him like a cold arctic wave had crashed down onto the car and spun him out of control. She was right. Everyone in his family was French except him, his mother and his sister. There was this other person inside him, influencing him. A person he had never acknowledged or knew existed. A person he had never met until this moment.

"I'm a French-man," he said out loud. The words still sounded foreign to him, but they made him smile. This undiscovered side of himself opened up a whole new world. Gave him a whole new set of options. He now had a door to open. He could stretch out and find himself. He could learn to breathe in French.

"I think we need to find a French daycare," he said.

"Yes, I was thinking the same thing," she said. "I'll look through the paper in the morning."

In the parking lot of their apartment Dan helped unload the baby from the car. The rain was now a light mist and it felt refreshing, it put a smile on his face.

"I'm going to get a coffee, would you like one?" he asked.

"Really, you're just going to leave me here," she said.

"I'll be right back. I'll get you one if you want?"

"I don't need one and neither do you. Too much coffee is no good for you. You're not going to be able to sleep and it will mess with your stomach. Just stay here."

Dan's smile was gone from his face. He clenched his teeth. He rolled fingers tight to his palm. There was that tone again. The same one he had been hearing all day. His eyes went straight through her. He wanted to put his fist through the car window. He wanted to get in that car, pick up a coffee, and keep driving. If she had been one of his male friends, she would have received a punch in the mouth by now. Even if she was his mother, he would have told her to lay the hell off. But she was neither of these, she was his wife and she was standing in the rain, tired and wet, frustrated and stressed, and she was asking for his help. He stretched out his hand and unclenched his fingers.

"Here, hand me those bags. I'll make some gross instant coffee in the house."

"Thank you," she said.

Dan watched as she trudged away, baby under one arm and bags in the other. They were both soaked from the rain, tired and wrung out from the day.

"Je t'aime," he said, but it wasn't loud enough for her to hear.

AT THE GAS STATION

Karen McCauley

Jane Smith climbed the hill, her head pounding with every step as the whine of the highway reached her like a mosquito in the ear. Already the day felt dry and hot and dusty, even at 7:30 in the morning. She could taste it. How much had she had to drink since closing at 10:00 the night before? How much had she slept? Not very much, but she was seventeen years old and, therefore, resilient. Sue's dad had reminded her of this as she crept out the door of her friend's house while everyone else who crashed there last night was still sleeping. "When I was your age I only slept on Wednesdays!" he reminded her as he waved a coffee mug by way of invitation to join him for a cup that she didn't have time to accept. Jane could hold her own with the older crowd she ran with, and she was welcome to crash at the homes of any of her friends. Parents always thought she was older than she was anyway, even her own. Because she had a job, and as long as kept her grades up, she had a degree of freedom not every girl her age enjoyed.

Cresting the hill, McNickel's Gas & Variety came into view alongside the highway. Gas fifty cents per litre. People were still griping since the sign was changed on Monday. The job was money in her pocket she didn't have to account for; and, more importantly, it was a 'get out of camp free' pass for the first summer of her memory. In this moment, however, she acknowledged a wistful pang, thinking how great it would be feel to be waking up at the lake this morning instead of serving everyone else on their way to holiday.

Reaching the parking lot, Jane picked up the pace even though she was pretty sure she wasn't late. The bundle of *Toronto Star* newspapers weren't all that was waiting for pick up on the doorstep. Beside these sat some kid; Danny Lachance, it looked like — Jenn's younger brother. "Here we go," she sighed. Not even enough peace and quiet to open up the pumps and put on the coffee.

"A little early for that first candy fix, isn't it?" she saluted.

"Jenny said to come," he mumbled without looking up from his shoes that were shuffling in the gravel and making his skinny bare legs dusty grey.

"Right," she sighed. And another happy weekend dawns on the Lachance family. Jenn's shift was scheduled to start at 10:00, once the opening routines were done and the traffic started to pick up. In return, Jane's shift was scheduled to end at 6:00 and Jenn would do the close. Jenn could be a pain the ass about some things, but she was pretty good about coming in early or staying later if Jane needed her. The "J Team," the others called them.

On her way to fill the coffee pot the phone started ringing. "McNickel's," Jane answered. Anyone who expected "Good morning," or "how can I help you?" would need to wait at least until she got the coffee on.

"Good, you're there," Jenny said. No "good morning" from her either.

"Is Danny with you?"

"Yes, he was on the stoop guarding the newspapers when I got here."

"Okay. Sorry Jane, but could you just keep him with you until I get there? I'll be in as soon as I can."

"Yeah, he's alright here." Then, she had to ask if everything was okay, even though Jane knew that the best-case scenario was Jenn was just keeping the house quiet so the old man would stay passed out until the nastiest part of the hangover was past.

"Oh sure," Jenny sighed. "Dad just got paid yesterday."

Enough said. Perhaps too much. Jane's dad worked as a miner, which was very ordinary around here, but also a relief. Jane was beginning to understand how to be grateful for a father who was generally reliable, came home when he was expected, never scared or embarrassed them.

Jane hung up the phone and looked over at the boy who had clearly been hanging onto every word of her conversation once he realized who she was talking to. Was he five or six? Certainly he was a lot younger than his sister, and small for his age.

The boy was wearing an oversized neon yellow t-shirt emblazoned with "Frankie says relax." Clearly it was a handoff of Jenny's from ninth grade. Already it was a piece of nostalgia that no one Jane knew would be caught dead wearing, not that she ever had. The child's pants were something between shorts and jeans. The old man couldn't bother to dress his kids even though there was apparently always money for a bottle. This awareness was new to Jane, and left her feeling paralyzed with the injustice of it all. She wondered if she would ever know what to do about that.

What she did know was that every cent Jenny made at the gas station was spent trying to purchase a degree of normalcy. While Jenny tried to dress up her poverty in big hair, shiny accessories and other trendy trappings of adolescent respectability, Jane obstinately resisted all of that, even though it was much more accessible to her. Standing apart was a luxury she could afford with her normal family and good grades. It made everything else that seemed strange about her appear deliberate, and also an expression of a free spirit, rather than a slave to orthodoxy. So Jane let people believe her to be clever; a fiction was just another of her lucky breaks.

Of course, Jane had heard the whispers that Wes Lachance wasn't even Jenny's real dad, but she heard more than she wanted whenever the coffee clutch convened on weekday mornings after the kids were out of the house, and before the good housewives of the neighbour-hood had to contemplate how to account for their day when their husbands came home from work. It may be 1985 in the rest of the world, but in this town that time forgot, more women were still at home than working a regular job; just one of the ways the town seemed to look backwards instead of toward the future, as far as Jane was concerned. Here, you were still either so-and-so's daughter, or granddaughter; defined by the legacy of past generations' indiscretions, accidents, crimes small and large, and occasionally their accomplishments. Jane's mother's steady and professional job (not a waitress or a cashier) marked her with a certain status, or at least held her aloof from most of the others around here; something that was sometimes a relief, and at other times just another source of strange embarrassment to her daughter.

Jane's mother was the secretary at a high school: one of the larger ones in town, thankfully. The local school Jane attended was still a forty minute bus ride away. She had spent all of her adult life in the "main office." As a result, she seemed to perceive herself as located at the nerve centre of adolescent evolution, which manifested itself in an all-knowing confidence about every mood, anxiety and resentment that her daughter ever expressed. After all, there's not much that hadn't crossed her desk in the main office. She also took pains to make her daughter over in the image of what she perceived most upwardly mobile, ambitious, and emerging young women desired. As a result, the back of Jane's closet was full of precious blouses, padded shoulders and even ridiculous knickers that were all the rage among the daughters of the mine managers who lived in the suburban catchment surrounding Mrs. Smith's school. Jenny might give a great deal for all of that, if she had a great deal of anything to give, but Jane insisted upon her standard uniform of big sweaters and jeans, and even track pants that were as ill-fitting as her mother's baffled resentment. Jane's refusal to embrace the fashion standard of having to lie down on the bed to fasten her jeans and avoid the washer, lest they lose their indigo newness, was not a concession to common sense. It might have made a difference had her mother ever really engaged Jane in a conversation about what she actually liked; but, more emphatically, her wardrobe was an expression of her solidarity to where she came from even as she was beginning to move away from it.

The tension for Jane was in her realization that she both was and was not one of those girls in whose image her mother tried to make her. She might be the only girl in her town going into the thirteenth grade, and then on to university, but she was also very much of this community. It was actually a relief for her to begin to work this out because it gave her a rationale, something to stand for. It took the crazy away. Having only a faint idea about where she was going after graduation made Jane more intensely feel her relationship with the dirt roads where she'd learned to ride a bike, smoke cigarettes, drive a car; the rocks she scrambled over to hide from the older kids, find the older kids and drink clandestine beers; the river that meandered through all of their lives and had places of calm and dark swirling eddies of danger. The intimacy of her relationship to her place intensified as her greed for language and the science that put all the cells and molecules together to make her world would ultimately remove her from it.

At other times her surroundings almost suffocated her, making her so impatient to just get on with things. Right now, getting on with things meant finally putting the coffee on, and getting a big drink of water for herself. She was parched. The night had not cooled the day before, and she had drank more than usual to revive her humour after her long shift, and to avoid looking forward to doing it all over again in the morning. This morning it felt like there was not enough water in all of Bass River to quench her thirst. The perspiration was already rising on the back of her neck by the time she finished unlocking the gas pumps. When she returned, Danny was perched on a stool in the corner, just watching her. As much as she couldn't be bothered with little kids, especially this morning, the boy's unnatural silence gave her the creeps. "Want a Freezie?" she asked.

Now he looked actually nervous, like this was some kind of test. "I don't have any money," he finally responded.

"That's all right. Breakfast special is on me. What colour?"

"Blue ... please," he remembered. Her own younger brothers could learn manners from this kid.

Jane fished two jumbos from the freezer. "I'll have blue, too. We'll have matching tongues," she said, sticking hers out.

Danny only nodded, silently taking the freezie. No chatterbox, that kid; not like her own little brothers who would drive her from the breakfast table back to her bed if she was out at camp, at least until facing the day became the better option to her mom returning to the threshold over and over, chastising her for not doing so.

Revived by coffee and Aspirin, Jane set to work straightening up: sweeping the floor restocking cigarettes, lottery tickets, and putting the milk cooler into some semblance of order. This was work that was typically part of the closing schedule, but Saturday morning was typically quieter than Friday night, and it wasn't like she was leaving the work for anybody else. Danny sat perched on the step-stool, watching for cars and giving Jane a heads-up before the bell.

At around 9:00 her first wave of kids swept through; about half a dozen boys who were older than Danny, but just old enough to be able to convince their parents to allow them to go to the river unsupervised. Casually cruel and predictably vulgar in their humour with each other, they sobered up considerably when they came around to making their selections, trying to get the best value for the bits of money that they had scrounged: ice-cream would need to be eaten immediately; a chocolate bar would melt to mush if they tried to save it; chips were all right for some, but boring. In the end they usually ended up presiding over the exotica of the penny candy and related Nerds, Lik-M-Ade, gum filled suckers and jaw breakers.

Even though the boys annoyed Jane with their loud lack of grace she respected even a child's right to deliberate over how to invest their income, whether it came from collecting pop bottles, birthday money, taking the risk of being caught swiping change from the counter, or if it was simply negotiated from a parent in return for some peace and quiet. As she was adding up licorice pipes and pixie stix one of the meaner, more stupid in the herd glanced over at Danny still slurping up the dregs of his freezie. "Hey, it's little Danny Boy," he sneered. "What are you doing? Did your sister dump you off here again?" Danny turned red.

Okay, thought Jane, enough. "In fact, while you little jerks are sucking on your candy rings and strawberry marshmallows, trying to drown each other in the river, Danny's working for me."

"Yeah, right," retorted another.

"I've been watching for cars," Danny insisted.

"Yes," Jane rejoined, "instead of using that stool to sort out the pop coolers, like I said." She hadn't said. Danny stood up, realizing that Jane was taking his part.

"It's only a job if you get paid," Wesley Cox, sniffed. He'd had less than the other kids to spend on his candy.

"And I'm paying him ... five dollars to stock the pop coolers." Damn! Where did that come from? Nearly an hour of her own salary, and she didn't even mind stocking the pop coolers. She could have easily impressed with two dollars. And why was she even trying? For some reason she didn't yet entirely understand, she wanted a kid, who had probably never impressed anyone in his life, to shut these boys down. It was too easy to take what you want when you're bigger and louder. When they'd finally settled up and left, Danny sat back down on his stool, relieved.

"And what do you think you're doing?" Jane asked.

The boy jumped up again.

"Those coolers aren't going to sort themselves," Jane observed.

"But I don't know how... "

"You know the difference between a Pepsi and a Coke, right?"

He nodded.

"Then start with that: all the different types of Pepsi in the Pepsi cooler; Coke in the Coke cooler. I don't know how they get so mixed up every day, but the pop guys get really ticked to see their product in the competition's cooler. Once that's done, I'll help you with where the

Orange Crush, 7-Up and the rest go. Then we'll figure out what we need to bring up from the basement."

And off he went, pushing the stool ahead of him. With the coolers at the opposite end of the store, across from the counter, it was a relief to see the back of the boy with his gaze turned to the task at hand while still allowing Jane to keep an eye on him. So the pop thumped in and out of the coolers, the bell rang for gas, the cash register chimed to make change; and the symphony of a slow but steady Saturday morning found its rhythm.

Mike Kovala was in early for his massive *Saturday Star*. Jane sometimes still babysat for him and his wife, Anna, more as a favour to her father because he worked at the same mine as Mike. He liked the younger man's work ethic and his activism as a health and safety rep. Sometimes the two of them talked collective agreement together over beers in the garage. Otherwise, Jane had mostly given up on that entry level employment, as her first generation of charges were getting older at the same time she started at the gas station.

The other reason she continued to sit for the Kovalas was she liked how they treated her; they were grateful for the service she provided and took an interest in her as a person. When Mike drove her home late at night, sleepiness conquered her characteristic reserve making it easy to answer his questions about her plans and figure out what she thought about the political questions of the day. In the summer he'd drive with the windows down and offer Jane a cigarette. Within the dark truck the smell of the wind, the smoke, and whatever came off of his skin was slightly intoxicating. When he left her safely in her driveway with ten dollars in her hand, she felt a little bereft, like she could have travelled that winding ribbon of highway, just talking and smoking all night long.

She recognized Mike's truck pulling into the parking lot now and had his paper on the counter as he came through the door. "You saw me coming," he smiled.

"No gas today?" she asked. Lots of guys filled up on the weekend so they wouldn't have to worry about remembering to work around the rest of the world's operating hours as they staggered through afternoon and graveyard shift rotations at the mine.

"Well, I was thinking about it, Janey," he admitted, "but you guys really do challenge a guy's local loyalty at the price of fifty cents a litre."

"I know, but where else can you get such personalized service?" she countered, placing a pack of Player's Extra Light, his brand, on top of the paper.

"Yes, there's that," he agreed. Mike hadn't planned on picking up smokes this morning, but wouldn't spurn the gesture. He asked after her folks, and she asked after Anna and the girls. They were looking forward to the start of his holidays and spending a day out at Jane's family camp. "Hey, maybe we could work that around your days off and give you a ride out?" he offered.

"Thanks, but I'll probably be working." Even though Jane missed the lake she, relished being largely on her own this summer even more. It made her a favourite at McNickel's for being most agreeable to switching into weekend shifts, and just about as many extra hours as were offered. It got so people more often expected to see Jane behind the counter than Lana or Lauren: the twin sisters who were Bass River's only employers.

Mike nodded. "Save up for university now, and then you won't have to worry about making ends meet once you get there," he approved.

Not exactly. Jane had every intention of winning an INCO scholarship, and she knew even if she wasn't successful her parents had always intended for her to go to university and would find the means for her to get there. Despite the periodic strikes, which punctuated her family's life, and all the other things they worked for — the boats, snow machines, the new garage, and her mother's addiction to redecorating — Jane knew the money for school would be there when the time came. The fact that she saved precious little of her own pay cheque testified to that confidence. The money she earned purchased her immediate independence; and this girl who thought she asked for so little was rather amazed by how much even that little bit cost once she stopped asking for it altogether.

"Have you decided where you're going to apply?" Mike wanted to know.

"Not really," she shrugged. Probably Toronto for sure, maybe Waterloo and Carleton ... I get to choose three," she explained.

"Anywhere but here, right?"

Jane said nothing. Why acknowledge the obvious?

"That's okay," Mark continued. "You'll be back. They always come back."

Jane felt the condescension, the patronizing tone. She was too familiar with it, but didn't expect it from him. "It's not that they always come back, but that no one ever seems to leave in the first place!" she shot back. Of course, that wasn't true, but neither was what he said, and what gave him the right to predict her future with such confidence? The satisfaction of the impression her retort left on his face was short lived when Jane recalled Mike once admitting to her of having nurtured his own dreams of university that his family had never encouraged or been able to afford, which was why he ultimately accepted the pragmatism of a trade, and a career underground. How many others never even contemplated going to school as an option?

"Right. I guess we'll see," he conceded now. Mike tucked the paper under his arm without drawing her into conversation about the headlines, which she had come to look forward to. As he pulled away, Jane wondered if maybe the only thing worse than things being so bloody predictable was when they weren't.

Jane was still standing in one place when Danny prompted her. "Gas!" The bell hadn't registered with her. By the time she walked out to the pumps the driver was out of the car squinting at the pumps. She glanced at the plate: New Hampshire. She sighed her exasperation with all tourists, and especially Americans who would ask her to translate the gas price into gallons, then expect her to take their American money. Of course, she did and when they complained about the exchange she stopped herself from asking why they didn't bother to have the courtesy to use a sovereign country's own currency. What kind of manners were those? Did they have any idea what a pain it was to complete the float at the end of the night with all that American currency? And then, "how far to Sault Ste. Marie?" Why the hell so many people would be keen to go to the Sault was a mystery that could only be solved by the presence of the border. Most of her Americans were dragging their asses home, dusty and exhausted after their exotic Canadian wilderness adventure.

His friendly greeting made her feel a little bad about her general bitchiness, and Jane resolved to meet his smile with her own. "How much?" she asked.

"Oh please, just fill it," he said. No conversion requested, but he hung right around, apparently inclined for conversation. When Jane glanced inside at the woman in the passenger seat she suspected it had been a lonely drive so far that morning. The tanned, beautiful and impossibly coiffed confection had her gaze set stonily ahead, not even registering Jane's presence when she leaned across the hood of the car to clean the windshield.

"That's my wife," he offered, almost apologetically. Like she cared. The car was nice though: a compact Subaru, all tricked out. The camping gear in it looked new, the canoe strapped to the top was hardly scratched.

"Where are you headed?" Jane asked automatically, expecting "the Sault." But now, the guy began rattling on about heading north: camping along Superior, the conference he'd just attended at Laurentian University. "I'm a geologist," he explained; and, as if that required further explanation, he added, "I study rocks."

"Well," Jane smirked. "You're in the right place for that." She anticipated the nozzle's kickback expertly and rounded up to the next dollar without wasting a drop of gas on the ground or, worse still, against the side of the car. There were guys in this town that would always fill their own trucks unless it was Jane walking out to the pumps. "Eighteen dollars," she announced.

The guy was leaning into the passenger door persuading the stone wife to hand him his wallet. "Want anything?" he asked her.

"From here?" Her eyes flicked onto Jane. "Do you have coffee?" she asked, speaking slowly in case she'd have to explain what that was.

"I was just going to put on a fresh pot," Jane rejoined cheerily, "if you don't mind waiting a few minutes." That was one of her favourite games dealing with nasty customers. The ruder they were, the sweeter she could get. Jane had shamed more than a few by the time she waved them heartily on their way, practically chasing them down the highway. Well, shamed them or convinced them she was some inbred stereotype.

"Oh sure, that will be fine," the guy said. Both of them seemed content to let the wife roast in the car. By the time he followed Jane into the store she knew he was a newly tenured professor, beginning his first sabbatical.

Jane thought he was going to follow her all the way into the back when she went to fill the coffee pot. "But you're from New Hampshire. Is geology even a thing there?" she asked. It was easier to risk a stupid question with someone you were never going to see again.

He actually shut up for moment. "Well, ultimately we all stand on the same rock, don't we?" he grinned.

Really? Jane wondered. The notion made her skeptical, perhaps because it was kind of reassuring.

The woman was pacing the parking lot by the time the coffee was ready. For whatever reason, she wasn't inclined to partake of the relief the store offered from the heat. When the guy filled a Styrofoam cup he seemed unsure what to put in it. Good marriage, Jane thought. Finally he just capped it and stuffed a couple of sugar packets in his pocket.

"Anything else?" Jane asked.

He glanced around. "No, I think that's all, thanks."

"Okay. Eighteen dollars then."

"What about the coffee?" he asked.

Jane shrugged. "That's okay."

The man thanked her and paid in Canadian currency without commenting on all its different colours. The woman returned to the car with him and they were gone. Jane wondered if they would still be together by the end of the sabbatical.

Danny had finished with the pop coolers, and done a pretty good job too. She told him so. She fished a five-dollar bill from the pocket of her jeans and the look on his face made it almost worth the expense. He looked hungry for the money, but didn't move to take it, like it was a trick where he expected it to be snatched right back from his grasp. "Take it," Jane said. "A deal's a deal."

"Gas!" they exclaimed together as the bell sounded again. Jane walked outside while the boy pushed the step-stool back to the end of the counter.

As Jane filled the tank she looked out at the highway and let her mind drift with the buzz of traffic. All that was strange and all that was familiar bisected this place where she stood and the location of everything she knew. Maybe if it was true that they all stood on the same rock then going away wouldn't really be quite the same as leaving. On the other side of the highway, a figure began to shimmer in the heat and take form as it descended the hill. There was Jenny who would always belong to this place — and Jane was glad. Things were getting busier and she could use the help.

REMAINS OF LUCK

Laura E. Young

The chocolate truck and the money truck collided on Highway 11 at 5:00 a.m., on Friday, January 13th, a morning that was bright but cold, sunny but icy, the kind of morning people felt proud to endure, while commenting strongly against it. We're Northerners, they'd say, unplugging their cars and tossing stiff extension cords at a snowbank. But at 5:00 a.m., the cars were still plugged in and hardly anyone was even up, let alone out on the road to witness the first truck spinning out. The armoured truck heading east to Ottawa from Winnipeg slid on black ice on the steep grade of the road between New Liskeard and Haileybury. The weight shifted inside the trailer, forcing the truck over to one side of the road then into the other lane in a bizarre ricochet.

It was all so hard to visualize except that the improbability was lost once it smashed and folded into a westbound truck carrying Laura Second chocolates from New Brunswick. Easter Eggs, hockey pucks, no sugar added chocolate, French Vanilla bars, and twoonies and loonies rose into the air, like a display of the greatest of the Canada Day fireworks, like the steam from the beating hearts of homes this sunny -40C morning.

Added to the improbability of the scenario was the fact no one was hurt. The drivers were neither critically, nor seriously injured. Remarkably, they would not ever suffer whiplash, not even months after the impact. They walked away. That fact should have been a sign something was off, but that, too, was lost in the unlikelihood of a money truck and a chocolate truck crashing into one another and spilling their cargo all over the road.

Most of the chocolate was deemed "ruined," so it was left for scavenging. The highway was closed to reconstruct the accident, but the curious and scavenging hopped onto snowmachines and quads to inspect the fringes of the crash site. As this was January 13th, some said they were getting an early jump on Valentine's Day. Besides, not only did no one become sick specifically from the "ruined" chocolate, no one would recall anyone getting sick at all after that accident, despite a long winter spent mostly indoors where other contaminants forced a person into bed, under a blanket and debating whether antibiotics would work in their case.

Then there were Susan's fortunes since the trucks had collided. That day she had been snowshoeing in the bush, freezing her face shut, despite the layer of wool she had wrapped around her head. Hell had broken loose the night before, and she had to get out. She had found a pile of money and, truly, she had meant to return it. But then one day rolled into another and it became harder to return it. Then she had thought it was just her luck, to balance everything else that came in January.

But now, cold and light were the least of Susan's worries. She was up early again on what would be a long June 21, when the daylight would stretch well past 10, even 10:30 p.m. Her brain couldn't care about those details as it was rapidly rearranging itself into odd quadrants: the first remembered that bitter day in the bush where she had been the one to find the significant bulk of the "remainder" of the lost coins; the next section was dealing with pain so intense in her jaw that surely she was going to crack her teeth just biting against it. A third part of her brain emerged into the harsh desert of denial, while the fourth quadrant said, clinically, speaking as if the doctor side of her brain was finally rising though it was too late to become a doctor. She was having all the classic signs of a heart attack in a woman over 50 and she had to stop denying it.

As she stumbled from the treadmill across the weight room to the women's locker room in the recreation complex, she looked out the windows south to Lake Temiskaming. The waters were deep and blue and surely hiding a monster. She always thought she had just seen it with the way the currents and waves rolled suddenly out in the middle of the lake. There was a lull in her pain long enough to distract her into wondering about Tessie watching over the sleeping Tri-Towns. Then the blinding jaw pain roared again, and again she was scrolling through the list of symptoms: all the ones she was trying to avoid if, say, for example, she really was a prime candidate for a heart attack. She worked out for hours every day to avoid this, the dreadful nausea. Now there was a heavy animal shifting, and then sitting even heavier as if it had finally found just the right spot on her abdomen.

"It's because I took the money. Just my good luck and it's all crashing down," she mumbled to herself as she sat down with a thud onto the wooden bench. "God, where is that chirpy, over-energetic gym staff when you need them?" She lay her head down on the cool wooden bench. "This is fine here." She was just going to rest a moment, let the pain go away. Surely this time it would stop.

In the meantime, Patricia had no paperwork to finish, despite all the responsibilities that came with being the Rec Centre Director. She had spent the past half hour casually observing Susan through the glass windows and walls of the weight and training room. Something didn't look right so she announced to the lunchtime crowd, all three of them, that something had come up and she was giving them a free pass to make it up to them. She had a pile of coupons for french fries but didn't think that would fly, coming from the Rec Centre Director.

The unusual was happening for Patricia and she knew to look carefully for it. But still she felt lucky she seemed ahead of the game, not just seeing what was happening but knowing to look, to judge and to get moving. Susan looked tired. Patricia had attributed it all to Susan working out all the time, but lately Susan had also been weaker on the weights too, hardly lifting even the pink chick weights in the light section.

Patricia sighed as she strode to the change room. Since February, as everyone around here knew, Susan's husband had been regularly visiting the new nail spa run by the Thai or Vietnamese woman in town. She was married to a forester who was out of town a lot. Denis was always taking this woman out on the snowmachine, in plain sight of course, but it looked bad to everyone except to Denis. "She's never been ice fishing before, Susan! Her husband doesn't understand. She can't talk to him."

Focus on Susan, not that fucker of a husband, Patricia thought. It was weird to Patricia how she felt like she was watching everything in high definition; as if she was seeing the heart attack happen. She watched blood well up behind the blocked, marbled fat of Susan's artery. It seemed like Susan's heart carried a black badge of plaque, like a maple leaf lapel pin so many Canadians had worn overseas somewhere on their person until it became uncool to be Canadian or to even be identified as a tourist.

Susan was on the floor now, seemingly with vital signs absent. Patricia grabbed the cell phone out of her jacket pocket; for once, she remembered where she had put the phone. As she called 911, she dropped to her knees, yelling at her colleagues, landmarking, lacing her fingers and noting how easy it was to remember CPR, 30-2, all the training came back. That was cool, she thought in the one detached, observer part of her mind. Wow, I just cracked Susan's sternum.

Susan thought she heard and saw Patricia — oh there she is — but she wanted more to think about Lake Temiskaming and how she was getting ready to swim in it at long last and how maybe for once, finally, the cold water wouldn't bite. The bright gym locker room lighting was fading down a long narrow tunnel as more people filled the room, everyone talking quietly. This was interesting. Someone is having a heart attack and they have to do CPR. She didn't have the energy to watch, she just wanted to close her eyes and listen. She heard yelling in a hollow: the rapid yet calm staccato of lifesaving. She was left with only one remaining thought before the edges around her eyes went bleak dark, like a thunderstorm sky: should I have taken the money? "I'm sorry I took the money," she struggled to confess.

"Oh, not the damn money again," Patricia yelled at Susan. She was now calling to her gathering colleagues to open up the AED, the one they had actually forgotten to check that week. Miraculously it was working, and they didn't have to rip Susan's clothes to get it on her tight, slim, spray-tanned core. Just lift her shirt. Simple. It took one shock delivered to restart her pulse long before EMS arrived, seeming to appear out of thin air. The two single, male paramedics were full of praise for the rec centre's CPR skills.

Walking beside the stretcher Patricia told Susan as she left the building with a pulse, breathing in a mask, that she should check out the hot EMS crew. Patricia looked up for a moment: the street was empty and no one would be around to actually gossip about Susan's heart attack. Oh, who knew it would be her? And, well, that husband of hers broke her heart.

Afterward, Patricia put ice on her burning knees and booked a massage to deal with the ache in her shoulders, back and chest from the hard compressions, as if she had pushed Susan through the floor to get the job done. "Excellent CPR" she told herself in the mechanical voice recording on the AED.

Later that afternoon at the hospital, Patricia sat beside Susan, who was lying semi-prone on her bed, wondering how she managed to look so well considering she'd just had a heart attack. "You were lucky," Patricia said.

There was a bouquet of red roses from Susan's husband in mid-life crisis. Susan stared at Patricia. "I saw you in the bush back at the end of April, that first sunny day."

Patricia nodded and recalled how, at the end of that January day, most of the money had been collected at the scene. The national media reported $5-million worth of coins in that truck. Ontario Provincial Police gave a stern warning to everyone that they must return any money they found. Everyone was speculating for weeks afterward about what they would do with the remainder. No one knew for sure what that amount was, as the police and other authorities at the Royal Canadian Mint were vague as the date of actual ice break up on Lake Temiskaming as to how much was actually missing. The Haileybury librarian ran to her computer and immediately penned a children's book about the day the money truck collided with the candy truck. At the same time, one of the artists on display in the library had drawn a few pictures. They collaborated and a publisher came calling as soon as the story came out in the *Temiskaming Speaker.*

Local editorials had speculated that the hockey teams must have found the money because a lucky loonie must have changed their fortunes for the better at the Provincial Playdowns. And so it seemed that was the end of the story, leaving the two trucks lost as yet another accident passing by on part of the Trans-Canada. Surely the government should have used the money to fix the roads, everyone said as winter melted away and spring gave its first reveal of the growing potholes littering the roads.

There were times after a long winter when Mother Nature took pity on the North and laid before the region a feast of sun, dry heat, almost blinding brightness. There had been just such a weekend in late April, well after Easter. Everyone had emerged from hibernation, blinking into the heat and swapping winter gear for bug jackets. With phones whipped out and aimed high for clearer reception, everyone tried out the app a couple of high school students had made to predict the trajectory and possible location of money that had been missed. Perhaps there still were riches lingering: gold bits, twoonies, loonies, under that snow-cone snow as it mingled with snow-melt mosquitoes. It certainly didn't hurt to dig around.

Off into the bush they tramped, spreading out like a search team looking for a missing person. Everyone found something that weekend. It wasn't much, nothing really significant, a lucky twoonie, a lucky loonie souvenir from that Friday, January 13th accident. A chocolate truck and a money truck crashing! Imagine. No one dared spend it and instead placed the coins on the mantle in a kind of limbo of not really stealing because we weren't spending it anyway.

"When everyone snuck out to look for money in the melting snow, I saw you. It's always hard to tell who someone is in their bug jackets. But I recognized you." She fingered the sleeve of Patricia's jacket. She always wore her shiny black rec centre jacket, like a security blanket or a walking billboard for community fitness — use it or lose it applied to the rec centre, as well as personal fitness. Patricia was known not only for being the woman who would not join her husband in North Bay, but for reminding people to work out. Sometimes Susan thought Patricia's presence made people not want to go to the gym.

Tears ran down Susan's cheeks but her voice held no hint of emotion. "I needed to tell you. The reason no one found anything much that day was because I found piles of it on the day of the accident. You gave yours back. I kept mine. Just my luck."

"That damn money is driving everyone crazy. People are still looking. I really only found about $100. Whoopee."

Susan smiled. "I found tens of thousands in a couple of bags. It was like a gift. I was sweating by the time I got to the car. You should try hauling money while you're hauling your ass on a pair of snowshoes." She noticed that under her black rec jacket Patricia wore a white turtle-neck and a gold chain. Seriously, was Susan now confessing to the rec centre director? She had been reading the paper at Death's doorstep, when Patricia had broken her sternum to make the CPR work. "Then all this bad stuff happened: Denis having an 'emotional affair' with that nail woman at the boutique."

At first Susan hadn't thought anything of it. She was busy and she had all this money. Frankly, she was done with Denis' menopause jokes when he was the one who was having a major menopause issues. Still, she couldn't believe how he had escalated from being a nice Canadian to the new immigrant to being the person who took her on a tour to Jamaica when her husband had opted out of that trip and Susan had to work.

***

Denis had tried to explain: they were like daughter-father or big-brother-little sister he'd never had. She was interesting, but that was it and it certainly was not inappropriate as he disembarked from the plane and handed the Thai or Vietnamese "little sister" back to her new husband. Fortunately, the forester had been transferred to Thunder Bay and they had moved in early June.

"All because you didn't want to go ice fishing or snowmobiling?" Patricia asked. "Not everyone up here does all that stuff."

"So I thought I'd have all this money to work out and take care of myself and it was my good fortune." Susan wiped away her tears. "Apparently not."

"I kept candy," Patricia said, desperately trying to lighten the conversation.

Susan laughed. "You eat candy, wow. Who knew?"

"Is your husband coming? Did you forgive him?"

"Yes, he's coming back. Yes, I did, but I don't forget. They're shipping me to Ottawa for more tests tomorrow morning. He wants to come with me. He's all scared."

"Did you want me to revoke his membership? Ban him from the gym?"

Susan shook her head. "No. Would you believe I actually gave him the money to go to her boutique for a man-spa day? I thought money would make it better for us. Let him relax. It just gave us something to fight about. And now I've had a heart attack, a real one, not just a warning. Or so they say. Who knows? "

Patricia's cell phone beeped. Her husband was back. She didn't reply to Reid, but she was mostly certain when she got home, he would have made her a strong cup of tea and would be heating a pad for her neck. She also really needed a workout. Likely she'd have to talk to Critical Incident Stress people. She looked out the window. It was the longest day of the year now, a seeming infinity of light. "I think we'll see the Northern Lights tonight," she said.

"That's a sign. I was lucky you were with me. Thank you," Susan said.

Patricia had thought she was the lucky one. Who wants a heart attack? That's bad, surely and besides, hadn't Patricia been motivated only by good thoughts of altruism and community wellness. She had decided any money she found would be used to purchase new lockers at the Rec Centre. Perhaps she could hold a contest and offer free gym memberships to busy moms.

She had indeed found dozens of coins along the path, a whopping $100 worth. Wow, big bucks. That would buy only necessities like some groceries or a tank of gas. Still, she had returned it all. Her name and the whole story went in the paper. She had found a decent package of Laura Secord hockey pucks semi-frozen in the snow. She had pressed the box against her heart to soften the chocolate so she could eat it on the mucky walk out of the bush to the road where she'd left her bike loosely chained to a fence post.

Then she began to notice odd, good things happening to her: she had never won anything in her life. This time she won a weeklong vacation to a yoga retreat in the Bahamas. Her husband, Reid, was able to go with her. He had taken leave from the base in North Bay with no issues or complaints. There was room in the budget for the new lockers due to some adjustment she didn't dare examine too closely somewhere in municipal funding from the province. There was money to attend a recreation centre conference. She was losing weight. She could do a yoga headstand without vomiting. And, today, on June 21, she had seen Susan have a heart attack in time to save her.

Susan grabbed her arm. "You know what I can't figure out is this. Who is the lucky one? Me, or you? Me because you were there for me? You gave the money back and so you were able to help me. I wonder what I'm going to make with this, me and my broken heart," Susan said.

Patricia stood up and hugged her. "I'm just glad I could help. You're the lucky one because I have to do the paperwork," she teased. "I'll see you tomorrow before you leave."

Patricia walked out of the hospital and drove home past the accident site and into New Liskeard, even though it was the long, roundabout way to her home in Haileybury. She wanted to see Lake Temiskaming beside her, over her left shoulder as she eased her way down Highway 11 B in the softly, slowly fading light. She hadn't been able to tell Susan what she really wanted to say. Patricia was going home to her air force officer Reid and another day at the rec centre hoping people would come in and work out.

Susan was the lucky one, she thought, as she parked her car and wandered down to the dock at her lakeside home. The water beckoned to her. The stars were starting to spin in the sky. Susan had been given her fortune and now she had to do something about it.

ISOSCELES

Tina Siegel

Polyamory seemed like a good idea at the time.

I bend the *Star* forward so I can see my wife across the breakfast table. Fifteen years ago, we were young, omnivorous and settled enough as a couple to admit we both found other people attractive.

It was a bit of a thrill, too. I admit that.

I don't remember who suggested an open relationship — probably her. She believed monogamy was impossible at best, destructive at worst. Unreasonable, was the word I think she used. I didn't feel as strongly as she did, but I didn't disagree, either. Polyamory appealed to my idealism and my bisexuality, both. It still does.

I'm not sure how she feels about it anymore.

It wasn't an easy decision, I remember that. There were weeks of negotiations, of discussions and debate and defining boundaries, that resulted in four rules:

Rule No. 1 – Dates are restricted to Saturday evenings.

Rule No. 2 – Both of us have a date, or neither of us have a date.

Rule No. 3 – Home by midnight.

Rule No. 4 – We meet each others' other-significant-others after three dates.

It worked for some time — almost a decade. Our rules loosened up as we did; the more confident we became, the less we needed them. Eventually, we replaced Rules No. 1 to 4 with Rule No. 5 — everything is negotiable.

There were rough patches. The six months I didn't have another-significant-other, and Trish did, for instance. That was hard. Or the year I dated Steven, who Trish hated. We weren't dexterous enough to balance such delicate scales, at first. But we worked hard and we figured it out. We were happy.

Then Trish's long-term boyfriend, Joel, moved to the UK. Date nights became nightmares — shouting and crying, occasionally throwing

SIEGEL 91

things. At first, I'd cancel my plans with Paul and he understood. He said don't worry; tell Trish I'm thinking of her. But it didn't help. Nothing did — not a trip to the French River, not a Joel Plaskett concert, not seeing Russell Brand live, not weeks of uninterrupted quality time. Not the trip to Europe she'd been craving since she was seventeen.

Finally, I gave up. I'd leave to meet Paul, and she'd be locked in the bedroom, or the bathroom, sobbing. Sometimes, she'd still be there when I got home; other times, she'd greet me with a smile and a kiss and how's Paul. Like nothing had happened. And that's where we stand.

I look at her over the newspaper again. She's still an attractive woman — small and curvy, auburn hair and bright green eyes — and I probably still love her. I'm almost certain I do. But I'm exhausted.

✳✳✳

Neil is staring at me again.

I sip my coffee, read my book. Pretend not to see. He's been doing this a lot lately, watching me when he doesn't think I'll notice. Usually on days when he has a date with Paul.

Don't get me wrong — I like Paul. We're friends, actually, and the four of us — Paul and Neil and Joel and I — used to double date. Last year, just before Joel left, we all went to Canada's Wonderland — none of us had been there since we were kids. They talked me into riding Leviathan, which has a 93.3 meter drop and gets up to 92 miles per hour. I hated it. Neil told me, later, I screamed the whole time. I don't remember that (though I don't doubt it).

What I recall is the way Joel and Paul distracted me by telling jokes while we waited in line, and how Neil gripped my hand during the whole ride. I sat between him and Joel, and I got tossed against one or the other every time we turned. Neil smelt like Old Spice. Joel smelt like coffee and cigarettes.

We stopped in Killarney for fish and chips on the way home. I remember that, too.

Joel moved to London a few months later, and things have been difficult ever since. I've been difficult.

I look at Neil from under my lashes. He's back to reading the newspaper. I can see the messy salt-and-pepper of his hair over the local news section. Below that, I know, is a pre-maturely furrowed brow, unexpectedly blue eyes and a neatly squared jaw.

Neither of us has brought up his date tonight. I suspect we're both thinking about it, though. I tell myself, as I always do, that I'll be calm this time. Reasonable. Myself. I won't throw a tantrum. I will not.

I finish my toast and pour myself another coffee.

❊❊❊

Trish holds the coffee pot up and cocks an eyebrow. I nod and push my mug forward. We make eye contact briefly, then retreat. We never come to the breakfast table without something to do, now; some excuse for the silence. A buffer.

Another senator has been caught claiming inappropriate expenses. The government has been caught helping her pay the money back. So Canadians don't have to shoulder the enormous expense, of course.

At least, that's how the Prime Minister is spinning it. *The Star* is a little less charitable: PMO Excuses High-Flying Senator's Bogus Expenses.

Harper must have had ten kinds of fit when he saw that headline. I smile.

Trish would enjoy the store — it would amuse and irritate her, and she wouldn't know which to give in to. I almost show it to her. Maybe we'd laugh about it together. But I don't. I drain my coffee, stand and head upstairs instead.

❊❊❊

I used to love Saturdays. Waking up late, then lingering over breakfast because there was nowhere to be. We'd finish a pot of coffee, maybe two, then put all the dishes in the sink for later. Then we'd lounge — on the deck in nice weather, on the couch in bad, always within kissing distance — and by the time we were ready to leave, we'd joke that we were sick of each other.

I assumed it was a joke, anyway.

I go to finish my coffee, but it's cold. So I gather my dishes and the coffee pot and put them in the kitchen sink. Consider going upstairs to get dressed, but I can still hear Neil moving around in the bedroom, so I go downstairs to the family room instead.

On the far wall, the one you see as you come down the stairs, is the fireplace. The TV is to the right of it, a group of five framed pictures to the left. One of them is Neil and I at Checkpoint Charlie in Berlin — he took me there a few weeks after Joel moved to England. Thought it would cheer me up, reset our relationship.

It didn't work.

Joel was emotional and artistic. Fearless. Neil is all wild intellectual leaps and careful analysis and progressive politics. Two halves. Together, they'd have made the perfect man. Or a balanced man, at least. Now, the whole world is off-kilter.

***

I pull on a pair of jeans and an old Clash t-shirt — I think this one was a birthday gift from Trish. Then I pad, barefoot, into the bathroom to brush my teeth. It's one of those days when I'm surprised by my own reflection, by the lines running from the edges of my nostrils to the corners of my mouth, and the crows feet around my eyes. By the grey, which is no longer restricted to the hair at my temples.

I'm 45 — not old. But it's close enough I'm beginning to see what old will look like.

I finish brushing and go back downstairs. My dishes are still on the table — Trish's aren't — so I clear up. Then I settle in the living room with a book of crosswords. Trish is in the family room — I can hear the TV — and I briefly consider joining her. Just sitting together, in the same space, for a while. It would have been a relaxing way to spend an afternoon, once.

Putting her own dishes away and leaving mine on the table was just petty.

Two across: was a copycat, four letters.

***

There's nothing worthwhile on TV. I turn it off and lean back.

I've never believed in monogamy — it isn't natural, that's why so many marriages fail. It's an archaic, misogynistic institution that encourages us to treat our partners like property. Nobody can fulfil all your needs for the rest of your life, and it's unfair to expect it. Most other primates are polyamorous, why not us?

And, when you do it right, it's fun.

We tried to explain it to our friends, and they tried to understand. Asked a few hesitant questions, made some awkward jokes. But whenever I mentioned Joel, any details about our relationship, they'd get nervous. Grin uncomfortably, look past me instead of at me. And they'd change the subject as soon as they could.

So I stopped talking. I pretended Neil was the only man in my life, and I was the only woman in his. Half my life. Half my heart. Half hidden.

I didn't mind, at first. Neil and Joel took up so much of my time, and it was exciting, the way sneaking out at midnight is exciting when you're sixteen. But now, I wish someone knew where I was. My friends have lost track of my romantic life, and I can't imagine how I'd orient them now. It's lonely.

I suppose orienting myself would be a start.

Neil tried to talk to me after Joel left. I tried to answer, but could never get past three or four syllables. I'm fine. I miss him. It'll be okay. Nothing else would come out, however badly I wanted it to.

There's a copy of *THIS Magazine* on the coffee table in front of me. I pick it up and start leafing through it.

Sometimes I feel like I'm 12 instead of 42.

❋❋❋

Trish dealt with the polyamory better than I did, at first — perhaps because I've always dated men, and she didn't see them as competitors in the conventional way.

I, on the other hand, had a hard time seeing her dates as anything other than threatening. She spent a lot of time reassuring me in those early days. A lot of time adjusting to my insecurity.

Down 7: burst of bad temper, seven letters.

We started to debrief after our dates. We'd discuss and describe them until every detail had been rehashed and nothing was left to the imagination. Sometimes that helped, sometimes it didn't. It took a long while for me to enjoy the funny, sexy, occasionally ridiculous stories she'd tell.

Well, I didn't mind the ridiculous ones so much.

Once – it was one of the first dates she went on — the guy showed up thirty minutes late and drunk. He apologized and asked for a kiss. She said no, and he sat down. He asked for a kiss again. Again, she said no. He kept asking. She left, sticking him with the bill for the two drinks and the fries she'd had while she waited.

So I didn't get much practice dealing with a jealous Trish — if she is jealous, and not just grieving, which I don't have much practice with either. She's generally the even-keeled one, and I can't seem to steady her.

***

Anarchy in the Nunnery: Nuns fight for a more progressive, inclusive, egalitarian Catholic Church.

Lost Girls: The human sex trafficking industry.

Gone Huntin': Hunting as the next big local eating trend.

I read without retaining much, and keep an ear tuned to the upper floors. Not much movement for the past few hours. I glance at the DVD player, 4:30. Neil will be leaving to meet Paul soon. I want to go and say good-bye, have a good time, say hi to Paul.

Paul refused to date Neil until he met me. Make sure it was above-board. I thought that was sweet. So we had him over for dinner one night. We ordered in Chinese food and watched *X-Men: First Class* and talked about everything except relationships. By the time he left, he was comfortable enough to hug me and kiss Paul goodbye.

That was a good evening.

I put *THIS* back on the coffee table. Lay down on the couch. Close my eyes. Somewhere upstairs, I hear footsteps.

***

I finish most of the crossword, fold it up and leave it on the kitchen table for later. Paul and I are meeting at The Buddah at 5:30, which means I have to leave by 5:00. I glance at my watch. Ten minutes.

I put on my shoes and coat. Then I pat the pockets — bus pass in one, nothing in the other. Where are my keys? I look around. I usually put them in the little dish on the front hall table, but they aren't there.

Kitchen by the microwave? No.

End table in the living room? No.

I'm about to run upstairs and check my nightstand when I spot them — they're on the floor, half-inside and half-outside the closet. I pick them up and open the door. I pause, then call down to Trish that I'm leaving.

✳✳✳

Neil is running around. He's lost his keys or his bus pass. This doesn't happen often, but when it does they've either dropped out of his coat pocket onto the closet floor or he's left them in the bedroom.

I turn on my side so that I'm facing the back of the couch. The best way to get through date night, now, is to sleep through as much of it as possible. I take deep breaths. Concentrate on the rise and fall of my chest, on inhaling and exhaling. Focus so intently that there's no room for any other thoughts or feelings.

Upstairs, the hurried footsteps stop. The front door opens. Neil shouts that he's leaving, he'll be back later. The door closes before I have time to respond.

Inhale. Exhale.

✳✳✳

I pause just outside the door. My hand is still on the knob. I thought I heard something from inside — Trish's voice? So I wait a moment. Silence. I must have been mistaken. I pat my pockets once more and head west, toward the bus stop.

It feels like running from the scene of a crime, like a getaway I've been planning for months.

The bus is full of people. I take a few deep breaths and my shoulders loosen. There's a pretty woman sitting across from me — short, choppy black hair and blue eyes and sharp-cut features — who looks up just as I'm looking at her. We smile and nod and look away.

When I met Trish, she'd just moved from Dartmouth. She was born and raised out east, and it was a traumatic change, or should have been. Her family and friends, her job, everything familiar — she left it all behind. I asked her if she'd been scared. She shrugged and said terrified. Fearless, I thought. And it was fascinating, because I was afraid of so much back then — of myself and other people and feeling like a gawky adolescent for the rest of my life.

Trish has always been more confident than I am, or more out-going, anyway. She's the one who sat down next to me the night we met at Peddler's. She the one who struck up a conversation, and she's the one who kissed me on the cheek and slipped her number into my hand as she left.

That had never happened to me before. It took me a while to realize I'd been picked up. Imagine my surprise when it happened again at Starbucks a week later.

Of course, Trish is also less flexible. Left to herself, she'd eat the same food and read the same authors over and over again. She'd go to the same cafe, use the same purse, buy the same running shoes. Convincing her to change generally requires bribery or subterfuge. The one flaw in an otherwise perfect character, she says.

She does regularly eat Vietnamese because it's my favourite, though.

The pretty woman gets off two stops before I do.

***

I'm hungry. I try to picture what we have in the fridge that I could turn into a meal.

On the other hand, I could also order pizza.

Neil used to have this cat. Ginny. I'm a dog person, but Ginny turned me. She had the funniest way of stalking shadows on the wall. When she saw one, she'd sit in front it, sometimes for fifteen or twenty minutes. Staring. Tail swishing. Then she'd yowl, jump at the wall and run away.

One night, Neil and I planned a romantic dinner. We made gnocchi from scratch, set the table with our good dishes, lit candles, turned out the lights. Ginny lost her mind. She attacked shadows until she had to stop for a nap. Then she went at them again. We lit candles at least once a week from then on.

The first night I spent at Neil's old apartment, Ginny was unhappy. She wandered around, meowing, for hours. The second night, though, she ignored Neil and curled up on my chest. When I woke up in the morning, she was stretched out on my pillow, along the top of my head. I think Neil was a little jealous — she only ever slept beside him.

Then, one day, I came home from grocery shopping. I could hear Neil sobbing as soon as I stepped through the door. I dropped the bags and followed the sound to our bedroom. He was sitting on the bed. Ginny's little body was laid out on his lap.

The vet told us, later, that she'd probably had a stroke.

I haven't thought about Ginny in years.

I rub my eyes and get up off the couch. Maybe Chinese.

✳✳✳

Paul is waiting when I arrive. He stands, and I give him a quick kiss hello. Then I shrug off my coat, and we both sit.

About four months after we started dating, Trish and I had Paul and Joel over for brunch. It was the middle of summer — July, I think — so we took everything out to the deck and made mojitos instead of coffee.

It was ... not awkward, at first ... but crowded. Stifling. There were a lot of different connections and histories packed into the space between us, and I, for one, felt a little claustrophobic. I hadn't thought through the consequences of having two lovers, both current, in the same place at the same time.

But things improved. Maybe it was the alcohol, or maybe it would have happened anyway, but eventually we all relaxed. And when we relaxed, we clicked. Joel and I discovered that we both love Dostoyevsky. Paul and Trish teased me about the tribal armband tattoo that I got when I was 21 and still regret. Joel and Paul traded dissertation horror stories.

Over her third mojito, Trish winked at me. I winked back.

I wonder what she's doing now.

✳✳✳

Joel and I were waiting for pizza when it ended.

We were at his condo, curled up on the couch talking and half-watching the news. Holding hands loosely. I asked him how work was going, and he got very quiet. He turned off the TV. My heart jumped into my throat and my stomach dropped to the floor. We stared at each other for a minute or two. I knew, but he said it anyway. They're moving me. London. Next month.

I left my hand in his. Stared straight ahead and opened my mouth, then closed it. Joel didn't say anything either, so we just sat there. I remember thinking I should leave over and over again. And then stand, and go. Then I'd think this is the last time and I'd stay.

If you ask me, the pizza came an hour later, but it was probably ten, maybe fifteen, minutes. Joel answered the door. By the time he paid, I had my shoes and coat on. I said I love you and left.

I've never told Neil any of that.

✽✽✽

I don't want to go home.

This isn't a new thought, since Joel left, but it's the first time I've articulated it so precisely. I almost say it out loud, to Paul, but he's telling me about this book he's reading and he's so enthusiastic I don't want to interrupt him.

I don't know what happened that night. I could never get Trish to talk about it in anything but general terms. All I know is that I'd been home from my date for about ten minutes — Paul and I had gone to a movie, I think — when I heard her keys in the front door.

I was putting on the boxers I wear to bed. I looked up, and she was standing in the door of the bedroom. Her eyes were wide and wet, and one hand was clamped over her mouth. I thought someone was dead. She gave one loud sob, then came over and leaned against me. I kissed the top of her head. Joel is leaving, she finally said.

That was a restless night for both of us. Trish was up and down, up and down — sometimes she'd go downstairs to the kitchen, other times just to the bathroom for a drink of water — and I half-woke up every time the mattress shifted.

The next morning was quiet. Neither of us were alert enough to make conversation, and I wouldn't have known what to say anyhow. Trish just ate her breakfast, then went out on the deck with her coffee. She didn't say a word, and that's where she stayed until dinnertime.

It's been like that ever since — I can't figure out what to say, and she won't say anything. The only time post-Joel that's felt normal was our visit to Berlin. We spent four days there — visited artists' squats in Mitte, toured the Reichstag, straddled the old border between East and West, wrote on the Wall.

Sometimes I wish we'd stayed there. We could have learned German.

***

Neil's late. It's 10:00, and I haven't heard from him, which is unusual. Soon, I'll start to wonder if he's coming home at all.

I got lucky tonight — I found a Criminal Minds marathon on Bravo that was mindlessly gory enough to distract me. I even dozed off for a while, but I also made sure my cell phone was within reach the whole time. And I double-checked the volume on the ringer.

I almost call Neil at 10:30, to say hi. See how the evening has gone and when he'll be back. Or maybe a text message would be less intrusive. But if he wanted to contact me, he would have. I put the phone down.

The same thing happens a little after 11:00. And again at 12:05. At 1:30, I turn off the TV — just as the unsub is about to kill her third victim, which officially designates her as a serial killer — and go to bed.

At 1:40, I turn onto my left side and reach out toward my nightstand. I grope around till I feel my phone. I touch the screen to turn it on. Nothing. I put it back and resettle myself. Close my eyes.

I wish, for the hundredth time, that I could talk to my friends. But what would I say? My boyfriend has moved to another continent, and it's ruining my marriage? It sounds ridiculous, even to me. Poor baby, you'll have to make due with your husband.

Inhale. Exhale.

2:00 am. He's not coming home.

THE DUST OF MY OWN MOON

Lara Bradley

Tobi Shinobi had grown fat on the moon. Well not exactly fat with the Moon Nation's rigid caloric rationing system, just soft, pudgy. Even her face had lost its sharp planes and become a moon face — so common here — all round and flat.

She poked at her belly feeling her finger dip into the fold of flesh. She did it again, this time gripping the pudge between her thumb and first finger, squeezing it hard, before shrugging on her green space suit.

Her round belly made her feel bad. Life with little gravity, no matter how many hours in the Exo-room, made you mushy. Not that she had gone recently to the Exo. She couldn't remember when she had gone last. Moon days. Moon days muddled you up.

At first she kept trying to do the math to convert the Moon Nation days into Earth ones but soon lost count. Was it 27.5 or 29.5 Earth days that technically fit into one lunar day and night? Too long for anyone to wrap their heads around, Moon Nation had decided on the creation of a "Moon Day" with a 28 hour clock. What people on Earth would give for four extra hours in the day! The brochure had made it sound so logical: 10 for working, eight for sleeping, and 10 for ... for ... what did she do in those hours?

The first taikonaut women had been glorious; pearls set against the blackness of space. She had prayed with each beat of her six-year-old heart to be one of them. No rat or pet rabbit for her, all Tobi wanted was to watch the taikonauts and pretend to be one of them, too.

Black glossy hair cut in the same swish forward slant, Taiku and Pika had captured many hearts with their symmetrical faces, slender space boots, and luminescent skin. They were perfect and picked according to the rules: no scars, no scent, and one child (a boy of course) each. The women kissed their children's foreheads (the boys adoring and in awe of the machine behind Mommy), kissed their husbands' tense mouths, all thin and linear, and ascended into space, into history, and eventually onto the poster taped above Tobi's bed.

Those rules had faded away by the time Tobi's mother sent her application in to Moon Nation. It needed workers and lots of them. Younger and younger taikonauts each year, it seemed.

MN accepted Tobi — then an 86-pound gymnast — with scars on her knees. Tobi also had scent, as much as she tried to wash, wash it away. She smelled understandably of ginger and garlic, but also inexplicably of the sharp bitter tang of dandelion. It didn't matter. Moon Nation took all the young girls and boys willing to put on the uniform and fly to the stars, even those who smelled of weeds growing in the cracks of sidewalks.

She pulled on her thick boots and then bounced up to grab one of the helmets off the shelf — the knob of another girl's elbow knocking into her. She didn't say anything nor did Tobi. They had two minutes to finish dressing before the airlock lifted. Helmets screwed on, the teens surged forward to pick up their tools.

The worst thing about the moon, thought Tobi, not for the first time as she entered the airlock, was the absence of colour. Sure there was fake colour, things painted with chemicals found in a can to look a certain way, but not the kind of chlorophyll infused colour found in growing things or the rainbow sheen of a pigeon's wing. Humans weren't made to live without colour. You got to crave it as you craved so many other things on the Moon.

At first the MN uniforms were silver, like the skin of a new truck. That mistake quickly became apparent. The biggest danger working on the Moon is being left behind or drifting away. The silver of the first suits had made the bodies hard to find. They still found those adult-sized taikonauts from the early days in their silver suits.

One time Tobi had almost pressed her drill into one of them, face down in a crater. Turning the body over and brushing the Moon dust from the visor, a woman's grey eyes stared unblinking into Tobi's own. Could it be Pika? She had never returned from her last mission. Tobi thought of alerting Command for a pick-up, but didn't. Just put her back where she had chosen to lie, wondering if she should curl up beside her.

Decompression complete, the air lock hissed open. Lightened to the Moon's gravity, the teen taikonauts bounced forward, lining up by colour and job — the greens, then yellows, blues, and finally the reds. Grey dust puffed up from their boots, dulling the brightness of their suits.

Then the Earth slipped into view. Everyone. Stopped. Their heads swiveling to it as one, drinking down its blue and faint traces of green; there was so much more brown on it now though, wasn't there?

Had the park near her old home died off too? Tobi had taken her brother Bo there each morning at daybreak, before the sun's heat had made it unbearable, to play among its bamboo. Their last visit, the bamboo had seemed to take on a yellowish tinge, she thought, still staring, still drinking in the Earth hanging-up there in the black.

Bzzt. Command had gotten wise to this time sucking problem of colour thirst and had installed electrical pressure points within the suits. Little buzzes of pain prodded the teens back into movement.

Tobi launched herself onto the back of the Silverado Transporter with the other greens. One of the boys bashed into her with his drill. He didn't apologize over the intercom.

I want to go home. The thought came so quickly and fiercely, she couldn't stop the tears. Her suit responded, suctioning them away.

She didn't know anyone who had made it back, who said their goodbyes before heading home. The faces she remembered from her shuttle to MN were mostly gone — assigned to new colours or among those who had stayed out and not returned to the airlock. Was today the day? She tasted the idea.

Tobi's contract was for three years. But how many had passed? Surely four. That made her 17 no 18 now. They would have to release her. Tobi pressed the intercom button.

"Command, when can I go home?"

"Focus on your work Tobi Shinobi."

"Command how long have I been here?"

Muffled swearing over the line.

"Why do they ... the answer has not changed since yesterday Ms. Shinobi. It's been 2 years. Moon Nation years."

Could she be only 16? She felt dried out and old as the dust of her own moon.

The Silverado stopped and one by one the greens jumped — arcing high against the shards of stars and then sending up clouds of grey when their boots planted down. A glitter globe with the dullest glitter imaginable.

Tobi pitched herself ass over heels off the Silverado. Earth spun beside her, steadying her as she landed. Tobi swallowed its burst of blueness, feeling it expand and fill her. For a timeless moment she could taste its salty air and smell the sun-fed tang of dandelions.

Tobi laughed. She ached to dunk her head into its oceans, run her fingers through its trees and slide down its icy mountains feeling the wind tangle her hair. When was the last time wind touched her skin? That's right. Just before the launch when the sun warmed the backs of her calves and the wind raised bumps along her arms, as she walked across the tarmac with her brother and mother before suiting up.

Buzzzzzz. A long buzz this time. The pain spread from her core into the tips of her fingers and down the backs of her legs, arching to her toes. Pain wasn't the right word for it. Hurt. Hurt just a bit stronger than the pain of being, being here on the Moon. A good-strong pain that woke you up and made you move.

Time to work.

She looked away from the Earth and down at her drill. Flecks of lunaboreum caught the light.

What had her mother said when she left?

"There is nothing for you here. Go. Go be like Taiku and Pika. Only lunaboreum can save us now."

No, no, no that was the mother from last night's movie. Movie or newsie? Straight backed, with a shiny breathing tank back-packed to her shoulders, and the smog of the city billowing around her. As she said farewell to her daughter, a close-up showed her black eyes, enlarged by tears.

Tobi used to have dark eyes. But they too had lightened to match the same colourless dust around her.

Moon muddled again. There was something she had to do, to do with this drill in her hand.

"Tobi, line up with the others," said Command.

The greens stood arms-length apart ready to jump forward into the crater. Always first, they were the breakers of the surface. Behind her, she didn't have to turn around to know that yellows stood ready with their shovels, then a line of blues with their hover-boxes. And finally the reds or "lobsters" with their scoop-shaped gloves needed to feed the moon rocks, lunaboreum really, into the machine.

Her real mother had been for the most part silent seeing Tobi off. Her head bowed and eyes avoiding Tobi's, holding tightly to Bo's hand. He was consumed by the sight of the rocket ship, straining forward to try to touch its metallic flanks before it filled with the fire that would send Tobi into space.

"Only three years," her mother whispered.

"Only three Moon Nation years," Tobi answered, looking at her younger brother with his new breathing tank.

Moon Nation had brought the lunaboreum right to their house as part of Tobi's blood bonding. A pinprick and a smudge on the tablet and the next three years, Moon Nation ones, signed away.

Recruiter Ken laughed when her mother brought him to her bedroom to see the now grayed and soot-smudged poster of the taikonauts.

"Taiku and Pika," he said, running his finger along Pika's inner thigh. "Good campaign but I guess we don't need them anymore ... It's all about family now."

He ruffled Bo's hair. Her mother took a deep breath, holding it in tightly for many heartbeats before letting go.

"Do you want to be like your sister and go to the moon?"

"Please, please, please," said Bo. "Can I go with Tobi? I'll — "

"Bo, no. You need to look after Mom."

There was enough lunaboreum in the packet, flipped casually onto their kitchen table by Recruiter Ken, to last her brother for years. Bo would get the chance to live to Tobi's age.

Her mother's tank was only a quarter full. Enough for ... How did it go again? Enough for two and a half more years. Earth years. Maybe three if, she stretched it, sleeping for extra hours at night. Tobi might see her on her return. She said she would think of something and not to worry.

Reflexively Tobi looked up again to the Earth, wanting this time, not its blueness, but to see her mother's face. A face harder to remember — it kept blurring with the screen mothers, who might be all the same mother they looked so similar. Like Pika and Taiku but grown older.

"When do I go home again?" she asked over the intercom.

Buzz. Just pain. No answer.

She nudged the drill into the ground. Grey dust exhaled from where she dug in. It took little effort to break off a piece of lunaboreum bigger than her brother's head. One that would keep 20 people going for a quarter of a lifetime.

Child's play. No, child's work. That's what it was. Adults weren't suited for working on the Moon's surface, becoming muddled even quicker than the teens. Plasticity of brain is what teens have, Recruiter Ken said. Youthful enough to accept the moon's time trickery, radiation and other stuff, but old enough to ... to do the work, I guess. It was possible though, an even younger brain would be better at adapting.

"Forward three paces," the voice in the intercom said.

Tobi bounced forward with the others. Already the yellows had started shoveling. Shoveling up time for those back home. Tobi made a sound between a giggle and a wail.

A white rabbit hopped between the rows of teens and into the mini-crater she had started with her drill. Tobi took a breath, not wanting to hit it with her drill. Rabbits don't live on the Moon. Command was clear on that. Nothing lives on the Moon. Just a leftover dream. People had those here. Leftover dreams.

Was that a movie last night or a newsie? Something about an explosion ... how, even more lunaboreum was needed for those who didn't even have the sickness. Everyone now had the breathing tanks. Their work was saving the "people of Earth."

"Wasn't it all so amazing that this rock found on the airless Moon was giving breath back to people on their own planet?" the movie/newsie mother had said. All they had to give up was their youth.

The rabbit had visited her last night too. In her dream, it consented to sit on her lap while she smoothed its fur, humming to it. She had been happy to breathe in its rabbit smell of hay cubes and feel its soft fur.

Ding. The chime of the end of shift sounded through her earpiece. How had ten hours gone by already?

She had wanted ... thought maybe today was the day — the day to slip away. As everyone lined up, the dust made it harder for command to see. Yes, there was still time.

She would go. One, two, three bounds and she'd be down the side of the crater, look for the rabbit, and then fill herself with the sight of her mother. Not her mother ... The Earth. Fill herself on the Earth. Ignore the pain buzzer. So simple. So right. The plan complete, she sighed, filling her lungs deeply and readying to make that first bound forward.

"Tobi Shinobi you are to report to Central as soon as you have unshucked," said a voice in her ear.

Not today then ... Tomorrow. She turned slowly toward the Silverado. The boy ahead of her, now seated, stared blankly thinking his own Moon muddle thoughts. In his visor she could see the reflection of the crater they had just deepened and the Earth. Each day brought them a little closer to the darkside of the moon. Something white flashed in the reflection caught in his visor, something small and furry. Tobi jumped into the Silverado, facing away from everything she wanted.

Back in the change room, she flushed hot and then the chills started ... Moon flu. Great. Her joints now swollen with that familiar ache brought on from the decompression of being back in the station, she forced herself to finish putting her gear away and stumble through the shower-mister.

At least her head had cleared and no white rabbit led her down the hallway to Central.

Recruiter Ken appeared giant sized, surrounded by children. They couldn't be new taikonauts, could they? Maybe a children's club visiting the Moon? These kids, in MN uniforms, were still years away from puberty.

"Tobi! Meet our newest recruits," he said. "What have I told you about plasticity? Neuro-plasticity. That's what's needed. You teenagers are already over the hill. These will be our brightest and our bestest workers ever. These guys and gals are going to take on our biggest challenge yet, aren't cha?"

What parents could give them up so young? Tobi looked down at the cracked floor tiles. She imagined herself a dandelion growing between them, a crooked flower that didn't have to talk to anyone.

"Tobi. Tobi. Snap out of it Tobi," he said. "Dopey teens, huh, what did I tell you guys? There's a recruit here, you'll want to say hello to. He's following in your little footsteps, isn't he?"

Bo had grown, but not so much she couldn't recognize the tilt of his head as he pushed to the front. Would he throw himself into her arms?

Maybe this was what the dream of the rabbit meant. She would pet his silky black hair the way she had soothed him as a toddler when their mom was out.

He stopped, confused. There would be no hug. "Mama?"

"Come on man, that's your sister. The moon will age you up a bit that's all."

Tobi began shaking. At first she thought it grief. Bo's wasting of her gift — no her sacrifice — not to mention the waste of her whole being, ruined up here by the Moon. His own life would be similarly warped, unless the neuro-plasticity of his youth could indeed save him.

But no. Grief couldn't make you this hot on the inside and so coldly numb on the outside. Pure rage that's what it was.

"You aren't supposed to be here. You had enough for ... you're not supposed to be here. You had enough to grow up."

Bo was backing away from her. She had never raised her voice to him. She, who looked so unlike the slim, young gymnast who had left him two years ago. His sister, his protector.

"But your Mom didn't, did she? Pull yourself together Tobi, for your brother if not yourself," said Recruiter Ken, turning away.

"Recruits, come see where you are all headed tomorrow. We call it the 'darkside.' Any of you listen to Pink Floyd? No? Well ... Well it's the side that you can't see on Earth, not really darker than here, it's just we haven't gone there yet. And these scaredy-cats don't want to go."

With that he led them away. Bo said nothing, trailing the others and staring at her.

Tobi, spent, leaned her forehead against the biting cold of the window. The Earth was in view, but she ignored it. Her gaze pulled to the Moon's rough surface, where her rabbit joined the others in play. It must be play. How else can you describe rabbits hopping back and forth so ridiculously high? Bouncing up against the very stars, their white fur glowing against the dark. So many out there.

VISITATION

Kim Fahner

Greta was only ten years old when she began hearing the voices. At first, she thought her mum was calling her, but whenever she went to ask what her mum wanted, she was told she hadn't even been called in the first place. At times, it got so bad she plugged her ears, but that didn't work because the voices came from *inside* her head. You couldn't exorcise yourself, now, could you? Her parents ignored it, chalked it up to her being a Goth girl in a northern town. It was easier for them that way. In retrospect, she hated them for it, for not listening to what she said, mostly because it meant she suffered a lot longer than she had to. She remembered falling asleep in her darkened bedroom to the sound of the CBC, listening to the dulcet tones of some broadcaster. Sometimes, later in the evenings, the radio station would play classical music, and that often was enough to send her to sleep, so the voices were silenced long enough for her to rest. Her dreams were vivid, but at least there wasn't a constant stream of chatter or commentary going on while she slept.

Growing up, she was an outcast, often bullied and misunderstood. She once painted a forbidden midnight mural on the walls of the Elgin Street underpass, but as an adult she had managed to mask her weaknesses, her secrets, until the day she found herself on a railway trestle, perched over a deep gully somewhere outside of town. Greta had thought she'd heard a voice telling her jumping off would be a good idea, would bring her peace inside, would transport her to a place where darkness didn't live. The only thing that stopped her, that time, was the whimpering of a stray dog limping down the tracks further on, near the woods. The whining dog made her shake her head, helped her to come out of her trance, and made her think she just might be crazy after all these years. She'd gone, then, stepped off the edge and moved away, managing to convince the dog to come along with her, bribing it with a half-eaten granola bar she had shoved into her bag. The dog followed her home. Now, she had a black and white stray she named Panda.

No one knew she had tried to kill herself that day, when the sun had lit up the trestle like a stage. She'd just walked home, carrying a broken mutt, and continued on as if nothing had happened. Somehow, when Greta was at work at the local greasy spoon, she managed to keep a lid on the voices, to stop them from interrupting her life. It was hard work, dividing up your own mind so you won't crack under the pressure to integrate it all. That's why school hadn't worked for her, too much dancing around with other people, with the voices. It left her exhausted and spent. For her, the voices were normal; to others, they were marks of insanity and a badly broken mind. The gulf that existed between those two perceptions was wide, but Greta managed to accept that she was just a different sort of person, unlike others she knew.

✼✼✼

When she moved to Toronto, south from Sudbury, she'd found a roommate, Frieda, who was trying to finish her degree in art history, all with a view to becoming the curator of a major gallery somewhere. She tried her hand at art, with canvases spread haphazardly around the living room of their small apartment, but most were half-finished blurs of oil paint, with more paint ending up on the battered hardwood floor than on the canvases. One day, feeling frantic inside, Greta had snagged a blank canvas, picked up an abandoned paintbrush, and just started painting. Swirls of colour bloomed outwards from the pure white centre. Some looked like wounds bleeding out, or the beginnings of far off galaxies. The first piece, a mad melange of collage, oil, and even some bent chicken wire, ended up surprising Frieda.

"Jesus, Greta. Did you know that you could paint? When did that happen?"

Greta mumbled her response, tucked her dirty blonde hair behind her left ear, adjusted her glasses and tried to speak up. "Um, sorry ... I should have asked you to use a canvas. I just picked up a brush and it sort of happened. I won't do it again ... "

Frieda snorted. "Don't be silly, Gret. You will do it again, and I'll get you a showing if you keep it up. You've been hiding your light under a bushel, haven't you? No more."

From that day on, Greta found herself painting with frantic abandon. Frieda would come home from night classes at the university and shake her head in disbelief. There was one new painting every two days. At one point, Frieda wondered if Greta had forgotten about Panda entirely, often making time to take the dog for a long walk or pouring kibble into his little blue ceramic dish.

For Greta, painting was like therapy. It flowed through her, not from her. The voices slowed when she was painting, as if they got stuck in the thick weight of the oil paints, as if they had given up on destroying her. There was, though, one voice that kept speaking to her. She called herself Emily. "So, you should put a bit of green down that side there, and blur that bit of white with the turquoise in a swirl. Good. Keep going. Don't stop ... " Greta didn't mind Emily's talking, her presence when the brush swept across the white spaces, turning them vibrant and riotous in minutes. There were tall spindly trees, ancient boulders on a windswept beach, clusters of little red mushrooms amongst green ferns, but never human figures. In this space, in this place, Greta didn't want to deal with humans; they were too self-centred, too difficult to understand, too complex. She wanted something simple, something straightforward. The painting offered her that escape.

✳✳✳

One night, just past midnight, Greta couldn't sleep. She padded on bare feet into the living room. Four paintings were clustered together in a half-circle. For days now, she had moved one and then another, shifting them from place to place, bending her head a bit this way and then a bit that way, trying to see some kind of evolution in what she was doing. From the kitchen one morning, Frieda had laughed over a cup of peppermint tea and told Greta the configuration reminded her of a pagan circle of standing stones, like Stonehenge or something even more ancient.

On this night, the moonlight split the dark, casting shadows into corners and blessing the apartment as it washed the walls in white light. A shadow shifted, making Greta look over to the left hand side of the room. Frieda was asleep. She moved over to the bookcase to grasp a single brass candlestick, readying herself to confront the possibility of an intruder. Bracing herself, she heaved the candlestick up over her head in her right hand, her left hand extending outwards as if to ward off an attack.

Greta's voice trembled as she spoke. "I'll call the police, so you may as well just go now. There's nothing here to steal, anyway. We're poor. Just students. Nothing of value here ... " She backed herself up against a wall, thinking it might offer her some comfort. The wall would, literally at least, have her back.

The light moved suddenly as the shadow figure shifted to the armchair that sat beneath the window. Greta's heart sped up, her left hand fluttered up to cover her mouth in surprise and her right hand lowered the now forgotten candlestick. She yelped a bit, her mind not able to sort things out in a logical fashion. There was a woman sitting there, in the chair, under the window. Stumpy looking, her hair in some kind of weird fabric wrap, with the shadow of a dog lying at her feet. The woman's face was obscured and blurry looking. Something seemed to be perching on her shoulder. There was the sound of a single breath exhaled, spent out and then taken in again.

"Don't screech so, girl. I've only been looking at your paintings. They're not bad, you know. Reminds me of my own work at your age ... spirited, out of control, eccentric."

Dumbfounded, Greta just mumbled. "Who are you? How did you get in? Did Frieda give you a key?" Her rational mind searched for answers, but her heart told her none of this made sense. This was pure imagination, wrapped up in insanity. "It's me. I'm losing my mind again. Great. This is all I need ... just check me in somewhere and everything will be fine."

The shadow woman laughed, throwing back her head. "Nah, you're not crazy. I'd know crazy. I was crazy, or so they said. Too many animals, I guess, and being on my own more often than naught. I guess people never liked an artist with animals. They'd rather have the high drama of Tom Thomson, the Canadian Shield, an empty canoe on a lake, and an unsolved mystery. Single men are so much more intriguing, aren't they?!" She laced the words with sarcasm. "No. They didn't like Woo at all, and he was really my best companion ... "

The realization hit Greta squarely in the gut. This was no imagined voice inside her head. This was Emily. No, not just Emily, but Carr as well. How could that be?

"Okay," Greta spoke now more to herself than to the ghost woman in front of her. "So, I'm delusional, seeing things, hearing voices, painting like a possessed person, and now there's a woman, a dog, and a potential monkey in my armchair. How does that work?"

Another laugh from Emily. She shook her head, lifting her hand and pointing to the piece that was farthest from her. "Nah, they're not mine. They're yours. I wouldn't put them in that order, though. Try putting that one on the end there somewhere in the middle, maybe? Watch how the paintings move, how they'll shift meanings and blur into a larger landscape of the mind. Ever do this before? Paint and then arrange?"

Greta sank down into a nearby pressed wood chair, trying to sit herself up straight and take deep breaths. "My grandmother always said I was a bit psychic, a bit fey she said, but I never believed her, until now ..."

"C'mon, girl. Get with it. I'm asking you a question. You need to answer. It's only polite. Even I know that!" The shadow Emily spoke sternly now.

Greta jumped a bit at the scolding tone. It reminded her of her mum's voice when she was in trouble. "Sorry. I'm just a bit off tonight. Um, no, I've never painted before. Only just in the last few weeks. It's a bit overwhelming, to be honest. It just starts and it's hard to stop it."

Emily sighed, letting her hand drop down to rest in her shadow lap. "I know what that's like, my girl. You can't begin to rest, to think, to feel anything other than the sweep of paintbrush on canvas, when what you'd like more than anything else is to make a mug of tea and feel the heat on your hands, to prove to yourself you're still here, still alive, not crazy."

Greta nodded. "Yes. That's exactly what it's like."

A few more minutes of conversation and the shadowy figure of Emily faded, leaving Greta shaking her head in disbelief. It must have been a delusion of sorts. Her shrink would say it was a psychosis or something. Still, maybe it wasn't that, but rather a real visitation from beyond. Was one worse than the other? Doubtful, she thought, because both would set a person off and make her wonder about her own sanity.

***

After a few hours of pacing through the small apartment, waiting for dawn to break, and then drinking a few cups of coffee, Greta threw on a coat, leashed Panda, and took herself out into the elements. The wind swept dead leaves around the neighbourhood like worn confetti. She made her way to Ella, a friend who claimed to be a bit psychic. Knocking on Ella's front door, Greta found herself shaking her head. How had she come to find herself here, of all places?

The door swung open, revealing Ella with a mug of hot coffee. "Having problems, eh? C'mon in."

Greta rushed into the vestibule, took a deep breath of incensed air, and slammed the door behind her. "It's fierce out there today." Ella waited, nodded toward the kitchen and led the way there, offering Greta coffee. After a few moments, once she had sat herself down in a kitchen chair, Greta found her voice. "I've been seeing things, but this time I think it's for real. I think I'm seeing real dead people."

Ella snorted. "As opposed to fake dead people, Gret? This doesn't surprise me. How long have I been telling you, you aren't crazy. You're actually tuned in to things that other people aren't aware of just now? So ... who showed up? Dead grandma? Really dead ancestors? Do tell!" She got more and more excited in anticipating Greta's story. Greta just shook her head.

Greta sat there, pulling her chair in close to the round table and hooking her feet around its spindly legs. Panda, sensing her anxiety, curled up next to her feet. She sighed and shook her head. "Um, Emily Carr? It doesn't make any sense, but it sure as hell looked like her. A dog with her. A monkey. Woo, she called the monkey. That fits, right, historically speaking? Still, why the hell would I attract her? I only know her from the calendars my mum used to buy and put up in the kitchen back home. There were lots of trees and totem poles. That's about all I know."

Ella snorted again, laughing out loud, and then lit up a cigarette. "Sweetie, you don't choose who comes in to see you. They are just somehow, I don't know, drawn to you, I guess. What have you been up to that Emily Carr would like? Taking in stray animals? Didn't you save Panda? And painting?"

Greta shook her head in denial. "Ella, come on! How do I get her to move along?"

Ella smiled, then blew a giant smoke ring up into the air above her head. "She likes you. I guess you might remind her of herself. Consider yourself lucky. If I were you, I'd just talk to her, let her know you're aware of who she is, and ask her politely to move along."

Greta sighed, out of other options. "You really think that will work? I'm desperate, so I'll try it." The conversation drifted then, moving on to other things, until Greta left an hour later, determined to have it out with Emily.

✱✱✱

Closer to dawn than midnight, Greta lit up some candles and incense, and then began painting in her attempt to hopefully entice Emily to make an appearance. A short time later, Emily shimmered into existence. She was alone this time, without animals, and perched on the windowsill. She spoke first, breaking the silence.

"I know you want me to go, and I'm alright with that. As long as you promise to keep painting."

Greta couldn't believe she was having another conversation with the ghost. "I don't want to offend you. Not at all. I just need to try and get a better sense of who I am, and seeing your ghost around my apartment isn't necessarily a very good sign."

Emily's ghost laughed heartily. "No, I suppose not. Not to worry, my girl. I'll be on my way. Just remember to take care in how you blend those colours there, so that they don't bleed so violently. Distinction is important. Blurring of worlds, while it occurs in art, shouldn't always show up on the canvas as often, if you know what I mean … "

The air shivered, shimmered, splitting itself open, and Emily began to fade a bit, dissolve, and then sparkle apart. Tall totems seemed to sway around her as she went, and branches of great trees swept through the field of Greta's peripheral vision, so she almost thought she smelled sea water, salted and drifting through the air in a wave of brine. In her mind, there was the sound of a crow calling darkly overhead. She looked up and saw it etched, feathered and free, against the pale disk of a summer moon. Then, suddenly, Greta was left alone, paintbrush in hand, in front of yet another blank canvas, about to begin again.

WHEN THE WILD PLUM BLOOMS

Eric Moore

The creek begins somewhere. He'd followed it once; a young *Speke* searching out the headwaters of a lesser Nile. His quest took him through stands of scrubby cedar and tangles of horse fern, past the remains of a derelict sawmill; spectacular tuffets of mouldering sawdust and piles of rotting slabs, the buildings sagging and settling into the earth.

He never found his Lake Victoria. Thwarted in the end by a vast, foul-smelling swamp — the water brackish and dotted with drowned jack-pines standing like great, grey sentinels. Is the swamp the beginning? Perhaps. Or maybe the creek's origins lie elsewhere; at a hidden spring; its cool, clean water bubbling and coursing along the cracks and crevices of an ancient aquifer on its way to the sunlight and new life as the creek.

The creek has no name. It is simply "the creek." If you wanted to be specific you might say "Willard Mouk's creek," or "the creek beside the old cemetery." Willard Mouk does not own the creek but his home stands on one of its banks and provides a convenient reference point. Opposite Willard's house, on the other bank, is a United Church cemetery. It is called the old United Church cemetery as it is rarely used. These days, fad and fancy dictate the mortal remains of the devout will rest easier in a more urban setting.

Still, every now and then, someone — an elder, usually — is laid to rest in the shade of one of the great willow trees growing along the water's edge. Its massive arms tapering to slender fingers, reaching down to gently caress the grandfather or great aunt lying beneath; its feet soaking in the creek's weedy flow.

Perhaps these old-timers have relations a plot or two away and, even in death, long for the company of family. Perhaps they were fishermen or the wives of fishermen and will sleep easier with the murmur of water in their ears. Perhaps they were fond of Willard Mouk. Whatever their reasons, these few individuals have chosen to take their final rest in this all-but-forgotten acre, which, with the passing of time, has become something more of the creek than the church. People no longer speak of "the graveyard by the creek." Priorities have changed. *It is the creek* now. The creek beside the old cemetery.

The creek is not unlike other creeks; sluggish, bulrush-fringed; alive with the reedy skirling of red-winged blackbirds. It twists and meanders some little way beside Willard's tar-paper shack, then corrects itself to flow — perhaps in deference to the neat rows of granite and marble markers — in an almost perfectly straight line beside the old cemetery before turning again and making one last, lazy zig-zag into the Spanish river. There is one thing about the creek, however: it is the best place in the township for catfish.

Catfish. Mudcats. Horn-pokes. Be-whiskered bottom-feeders. Eyes like tarnished *BBs* in their flat, broad-mouthed heads. Skin — *skin* mind you — creamy-slick and faintly aglow with something of themselves or the creek. Darkle-hued in shades of the deepest ebony, charcoal grey and chocolate brown; ivory-bellied below. Two-toned scavengers possessed of the pinkest flesh grown sweet and succulent on God-knows-what their groping, bristle-tufted mouths may hoover up from the mud and silt of the creek bed; above which they hang; suspended, silent.

The catfish come to the creek in the spring. Swarming in from the North Channel, up the river and into the creek in vast, opaque schools.

"The mudcats are up," a savvy, stubble-chinned neighbour offers in the course of a twilight conversation with the boy's father on the front stoop of the white-with-green-trim frame house in the village. While he, the boy, off to one side, not included, not excluded, listens.

"They're runnin' in the creek next the old cemetery." *The mudcats are runnin'.* The boy thinks this odd. Fish cannot run. They have no legs. No feet. Yet every spring catfish and smelts and salmon perform the impossible, running up creeks and rivers all over the township. The boy wonders how far the mudcats run? To the old sawmill? To the swamp? Beyond? Maybe *they* know where the creek begins.

***

They come to the creek at night; the boy and two men — one his father — for that is when the mudcats come; in the spring, in the night; when the wild plum shrubs that dot the banks bloom fragrant white and the bullfrogs boom and chorus. Drawn by the moon and a primordial determination to recreate themselves in the same waters in which they were given life, the dusky fish swim in from the big water, up the river to the mouth of the creek, negotiate the turn at the lazy zig-zag and enter the strait by the old cemetery where, a few yards on, the white, sibilant light of a Coleman lantern reveals the boy and the two men perched on the flank of the mirror-smooth creek; faces eager, bodies settled in an attitude of relaxed anticipation.

The boy holds a length of knobbly bamboo. *This was cut by a real Chinaman — in China*, he thought to himself the day he selected it from a forest of poles sprouting from the belly of an immense wooden barrel in front of the hardware store. *A real Chinaman cut this and another put it on a boat and here I am clear on the other side of the world buying it.*

The boy remembers how he thought those things and now he thinks, *are there mudcats in China?* He gazes up the length of the slender pole, twice as long as himself; his eye following it to the very tip and then down the sturdy green cotton line to the red and white plastic bobber which he cannot see but knows is there and he thinks, *my teacher says bamboo is a grass but I do not believe it. This is not grass. This is wood.*

The boy looks to the two men seated a few yards down the bank. His father, a big, hard-working man with rough, calloused hands he scrubs every evening with a special soap containing bits of pumice stone from a real volcano, holds a rod of solid glass. (The boy has suspicions about the volcanic soap and the glass rod. He wonders what kind of fool would climb onto a fiery mountain to scrounge for tiny bits of rock? As for the glass rod, well, how could glass bend? Yet his father is careful to point out at every opportunity that it is a 'solid glass rod' possessing 'great action' and, although 'a little pricey,' will, with proper care, last forever).

Attached to the remarkable rod is a Pflueger Summit casting reel — all polished steel and gleaming brass with wonderfully rich bits of something the boy's father calls 'imitation mother of pearl' adorning both ends of the crank. It, too, cost a fair bit of money, but the boy knows – again, because his father has made sure to tell him on numer- ous occasions 'poor people can't afford to buy cheap' —the Pflueger Summit is 'a piece of real craftsmanship' which, like the eternal rod, will be everlasting.

All of this means little to the boy. Although he enjoys the crisp *clack- clack* of the Pflueger as his father is winding in a fish; and he likes to watch the angled, metal finger of the spool-guide as it travels smoothly back and forth laying the fine, black, nylon line down in precise, even rows, he is quite content with his simple pole of bamboo — prefers it even. For as far as *he* is concerned — a child steeped in the television lore of Walt Disney and tales of Huck Finn — *this* is the proper way to fish.

The other man is named Lester. What the boy knows about Lester is this: he is even bigger than his father, with whom he works in the tire shop on the back street below the hill behind the Legion. He carries a trucker's wallet, an enormous, black greasy affair attached to his belt with a heavy chain. The boy also knows Lester is very fond of cream-puffs from the bakery on main street — he once saw him eat six — and he has very recently purchased a brand new spin-casting reel.

The boy can see the glint of the new-fangled reel in the glow of the hissing lantern. Bullet-shaped, it sits atop an ebony pedestal fixed to the smooth, cork handle of Lester's rod. He watches as Lester clicks down a button at the stern of the reel and casts out into the darkness. He hears the hollow *plop* as the baits break the surface of the creek and a satis-fying *clunk* as Lester turns the one-armed crank, engaging something inside the reel which, the boy surmises, allows the contraption to spin. He can hear the soft, whirring *tick-tick-tick* of the new reel as Lester gathers in a gossamer strand of blue-grey monofilament line blending pleasantly with the deeper and — to the boy's ear — more authoritative *clack-clack* of his father's Pflueger.

The boy thinks all of this in a trice, in a twinkling, and then he thinks about it no more, for all at once, through fingers curled around his blade — *branch* — of bamboo, he feels the first, soft, tentative tug of a mudcat. But then he thinks, *no, that is not right. I tell myself that it is one mudcat, but there might be two of them — three even.*

In his mind's eye, the boy follows the green cotton line from the tip of his pole down to the red and white plastic bobber, down below the still surface of the silent creek. Down, down, down to where the line is tied to the thin, metal leader; the leader in turn attached to the harness resting on the murky bottom. The boy remembers the day his father showed him how to fashion a mudcat harness: three number six hooks tied an inch or so apart to a length of the same sturdy, green line, loop at one end for the leader to clip into and a lead bell weight on the other to anchor it. He remembers the smooth, greasy feel of the soft lead weight in his hand and how the afternoon sun flashed on the copper-coloured fish hooks his father bent to a particular angle with a pair of nee-dle-nose pliers, handing them to him one by one by one.

The boy imagines that harness now — *sees it* — resting on the bottom of the fish-filled creek. He sees the three hooks, each of them encased from barb to eye in a fat, bruise-hued segment of purpley-orange night-crawler which he collects from the lawns of the white-with-green-trim house on warm, dewy evenings.

(The boy keeps the worms in the cellar, inside an old packing crate stuffed with sodden leaves; nourishing them with coffee grounds, tea leaves and assorted peelings, cores, scrapings and skins from his mother's kitchen).

He feels a second tug and wonders again how many fish are at his baits. (He has seen two mudcats taken at the same time, but never three. He thinks he would like to see three — would like to catch three). The vibration travels up the green cotton line, along the bamboo and into the boy's curled fingers. 'Mudcats don't bite like other fish,' he remembers his father telling him. 'They suck at the bait — and they're sneaky. If you ain't payin' attention they'll strip every hook clean as a whistle.' The boy remembers his father saying this, but he is not thinking about that now for the tugging from the depths of the black and glass-like creek has become more pronounced, steady, and the boy knows it is time.

He stands, bracing his feet, elevating the pole and taking up the slack in the green cotton line. He pauses now, waiting for another tug and when it comes he brings the pole straight back over his head in a smooth, graceful arc which sets the hook — *hooks*, the boy hopes — and snatches the fish — *fishes*, he prays — from the thick, turbid sanctuary of the creek bed. One motion, fluid and precise, has delivered the fish from water into air onto earth; and, in a few hours, the fourth element will be kindled in the kitchen of the white-with-green-trim house and the fish will fulfill its destiny in the bottom of a well-seasoned cast iron frying pan.

The boy is thrilled. Jubilant as *Santiago*. He races up the bank to where the fish lies flopping amongst scrub grass and milfoil. He sees that it is a large mudcat — two pounds perhaps — with long, trailing whiskers and skin the colour of licorice. He brushes bits of grass and dirt from the convulsing creature and prepares to remove the hook. (The boy remembers a time when his father showed him how to hold a mudcat. He gingerly grasps the fish just behind the head making certain his thumb and two fingers are firmly against and *behind* the two needle-sharp, bony spines protruding just back of the bellowing gills.

Although he has never been poked, the boy has heard stories from his father and Lester about men requiring stitches after being gored by a mudcat. The boy is not sure if he believes the stories, but he is willing to give the fish the benefit of the doubt).

The boy safely extracts his hook and carries the gasping fish to a brown, hemp feed sack — already lumpy with fish taken by Lester and his father — lying just beyond the ellipse of the sputtering lantern. He adds his fish to the mess inside the burlap bag and wonders if the fish know where they are or how they got there? He wonders if they have any notion of their fate or take any comfort in each other's company? No, he guesses.

The boy now chooses a large night-crawler, plump and sticky with slime, from a yellow-labelled tin can and returns to his spot on the bank feeling the worm slither and squirm inside his clenched fist. He strips his hooks clean, tossing the old, water-logged flesh into the creek and, tearing the new worm into three equal pieces, slides on the fresh meat, carefully concealing every last bit of metal. He wipes his hands on his trousers, straightens out the green cotton line and bringing the pole over his head in a smooth, graceful arc, returns his baits to the floor of the dark, muted creek.

The boy settles himself on the bank and looks to the stuttering lantern. *Needs pumping*, he thinks. He watches the frantic death-dance of a large, dusty moth relentlessly bashing itself into the glowing, glass globe and he thinks, *butterflies come out in the day and moths come out at night — to die*. He looks past the lantern to the two men — seeming giants now in the gloaming and faint glimmer of the lantern — and watches his father reel in a fish. He thinks, *first I caught one fish. This time it will be two. And the next, three. Even they have never caught three at the same time. I would like to catch three.*

The boy takes a sandwich from a paper sack. He bites and chews. He gazes for a brief moment at the sliver of yellow moon in the inky, night sky and with the vernal voice of the marsh all about him he thinks, *this creek has to start somewhere. Everything has a beginning. Maybe I will try again.* But he thinks this only for an instant for through his young, gripping fingers he again feels the first, faint tentative tug of a mudcat. *Mudcats*, he thinks.

BEST IN THE REZ

Darlene Naponse

Hurting Lodge Reserve held it's first *Dog Show* on a Monday. No one really understood why it was on a Monday, but it was perfect. Even ol' Fred came out for the contest and he was sober. Mondays are always boring and disconcerting. Either the weekend had eaten most people's souls or people were still on the road coming home from a Pow Wow.

The health administration organized the *Dog Show* as part of their Hurting Lodge Healthy Dog Days. The day was beautiful. The sun shone and the mosquitoes had decided not to come out and feast. The community anticipated the *Dog Show* for weeks. Rumours alluded to bribery. Members of Hurting Lodge Reserve adorned their dogs with ribbon shirts and beaded dog collars. Many shampooed their dogs down at the lake. Two cousins saw a member walk his dog.

❋❋❋

Hurting Lodge reserve has 457 members living on the reserve and 124 dogs. Many dogs have no owners and run wild in packs and hunt deer. Others menaced. The remaining entered in the *Dog Show*.

A small crowd started to gather. It was spring, so everyone wanted to be outside after a long cold winter. Sue and Jen were selling bannock and scone dogs. Lena walked around selling 50/50 tickets for her daughter's hockey team. The benches started to fill; even Zane and his lady friend sat in their lawn chairs along first base.

June Keen was one of the judges. Her moccasins had blown a hole by the toe and her mini chihuahua kept licking her toes under the judge's table. The other judges; the Chief who was out from doing weekends in jail for drinking and driving; Dr. Karen Birch who came home for the event (she teaches at some fancy southern university); and Ola, the nurse practitioner who is always wearing the tightest t-shirt and a push-up bra (she is very busy).

❋❋❋

Seven members of the Hurting Lodge Reserve entered their dogs in the contest. The stakes were high. An undisclosed cash prize enticed many participants. To be the Best in the Rez, in the *Dog Show* was what interested most. To be the greatest is habitual in the Hurting Lodge Reserve. The bragging rights and the winning trophy is a new normal that most people regard. When members heard Peter and his Pyrenees Wigwas was entering, they wondered what would happen.

Hella entered her bulldog; Susan entered her Landseer; Jack entered his German shepherd; Sage entered her cat; Juniper entered her goldendoodle; Peter entered his Pyrenees; Samantha entered an unknown breed and Elder Jesse entered her boxer.

✵✵✵

Sand started to blow onto the judge's table, they all put their sunglasses on. Samantha rode her bicycle in the outfield, while Easy chased her back spokes. Her long fluorescent ribbons sailed a fire along the green. The smell of mud and rotting dog poop did not stop people attending the show.

The judges huddled around first base. Elder Ted shared a story about the first dog on the reserve. It was a wolf who ran away from his pack. The wolf walked into the community and entered the healers' tent. The healer named it and his atonement for leaving his pack was to care for a very sick young girl. The wolf dog, which was named, but never called by his name, stood by the young girl day after day. She grew up and her sickness was always with her. She could not run, or carry heavy things. The dog dragged her from hunt camp to hunt camp, where she assisted the healer. The young girl died in her 20's and the dog that was named died beside her.

June Keen and a woman hand drum group belted out a new song after the story. They sang out of rhythm, but ended perfectly. June cleared her throat then read the rules to the community.

Rule 1 – You have to be a member of Hurting Lodge Reserve.

Rule 2 – You have to walk your dog/pet from home base to the pitchers mount, where the judges are, then walk your dog/pet in front of the judge's table.

Rule 3 – All dogs/pets to be leashed

Rule 4 – No drinking or drugs allowed

Rule 5 – All ages are eligible

Rule 6 – Play fair

✳✳✳

The first round was the only round.

✳✳✳

Sage was first. Sage's cat was fourteen years old and hissed and pissed on only old men. She inherited Waboose from her Great Auntie Sue. Auntie Sue named her cat Waboose from her love of rabbits. Sue had owned one cat and five rabbits.

Sage walked her cat up to the judge's table. Waboose had a stunning moose tuff collar and leash. Sage walked fast, she was nervous. Waboose started to sneeze. Sage slowed down. As they pranced in front of the judges, Waboose puked up a baby bird in front of the Chief. The tiny carcass was covered with bile. Waboose tried to eat the cat again. Sage picked her up and then the carcass and walked away from the judges. They did not complete the walk in front of the judges. Sage buried the bird.

✳✳✳

On the catchers mound was a small puddle. It had rained yesterday.

✳✳✳

Elder Jesse entered her boxer, Jim. Jim is Jesse's constant companion and walks beside her on every dirt road, hidden trail and forgotten road. He is notorious for running across the Rez in seconds getting his treat from Jesse's sister, Hanna, and then running back, before Jesse even notices him gone.

A 1989 Chevy Buick cruised by the diamond. Jesse and Jim the boxer walked up to the judge's table. The '89 Buick drove into the far end of the field and was parking to watch the show. The car backfired and Jim the boxer jumped so high, he landed on the judge's table right in front of the nurse. The nurse screamed and fell back and off her chair. Jim the boxer ran down the judge's table. Paper flew east and west. Jim turned and ran back into Jesse's arm. Jesse carried Jim home.

Judges and organizers fixed the table. The Chief helped the nurse up. The nurse adjusted her t-shirt; one boob had popped out of her tee.

The Chief motioned with his lips for the next dog to be judged.

***

Hella pushed through the crowd pulling her bulldog behind her. The bulldog had no name. Hella's bulldog took after her. They both bullied and barked.

The bulldog yapped and chewed on his leash. Hella stood in front of June Keen and looked down at her bulldog that did not move. June's chihuahua looked up at the bulldog with no name. The chihuahua stopped chewing June's moccasin. The bulldog let go of the leash, turned and growled at the chihuahua. The chihuahua ran across the outfield. June chased her. The bulldog kept still.

***

Juniper's goldendoodle sat beside her through every episode of the day. Juniper's goldendoodle, Seeker, rescued her brother Ken when he fell through the ice. Seeker ran a rope to Ken and then helped tug him out of the water. Seeker was tough for a goldendoodle. Seeker can often be found on the roof of her dog house, watching. A week ago, he was found on the roof of the band office, howling to the east. He climbed up by a truck and some old scaffolding. When it was time to walk Juniper a twelve-year-old ingénue put the leash on her goldendoodle Seeker and they walked past the judges. When they finished the walk in front of the judges, Juniper unleashed Seeker and Seeker laid down by her feet.

***

Two members of Hurting Lodge Reserve sat on the home bench and were laughing and looking over at Peter and Wigwas. Peter turned and walked behind the fence.

***

Susan is five foot four; her Landseer dog, King, weighs two hundred and four pounds and is three and half feet tall. Nothing around Susan is clean of dog hair. The hair from her dog is weaved so tight in her sweater; you would not know it was cotton a month ago.

The two hundred and four pound King would not move from under the bleachers. He was sleeping; he did not care if it was his turn.

Susan watched to see if King was breathing. She touched his belly, it went up and down. She pet under his chin and he snored. King's tiny hair particles flew over the baseball diamond. Beside King was Jack's German shepherd. Jack's German shepherd, Kid, has bitten more kids on the Rez than any mosquito. The German shepherd was a gift he got after he retired. He walked up and down everyday to the band office, through the high grass, across the makeshift bridge and down the valley. His kids offered him rides, bought him a scooter, but he wanted to walk. After chasing off a bear with his cane, Kid came into his life.

Jack and Susan, both widows, watched their dogs rest under the bleachers. They shrugged their shoulders at the same time. They ordered two pieces of bannock and two coffees at the Bannock Stand. They fell in love sitting on the bleachers, eating bannock and drinking coffee, near their other companions.

✳✳✳

Samantha and Easy were never apart. The mixed breed of unknown is the closest relationship she has ever had. Easy was both protector and friend. Mother and Father. Sister and Brother.

Samantha rode her bike to the judges' table and Easy followed with a perfect stride. Samantha braked at the judges' table. Easy stopped scratched himself and rolled in the sand. Samantha sat back in her banana seat, peddling past the judges. Easy stood up, shook off the dust and ran after Samantha.

The judges brushed off the sand. The Chief spit out sand. The catcher's area puddle widened with each participant. The barometric pressure dropped.

✳✳✳

Peter and his white Pyrenees were next. The most elegant and beautiful of dogs ever on the Rez was Peter's Pyrenees, Wigwas. Wigwas, the *white puffy one*, once helped pull out a moose from the bush. Peter had brought down a calf a kilometer and half down the red log road. The road was covered with underbrush, but had a small walking trail. Wigwas pulled the antlers, the fur and a rope. Him and Peter pulled that calf out. When Wigwas returned to the truck, Peter's new wife Sarah was standing by the tailgate smoking a cigarette. She saw Wigwas coming and ran in the bush. Moose blood covered the Great Pyrenees and he had a muddy face from drinking from the puddle. Peter and Wigwas's followed her for twenty minutes then lost her. When they returned to the truck, Sarah was inside and locked the door with her knife in her hand. Peter picked up Wigwas and threw him in the back of the truck. Sarah was always dramatic; the horror and gore were now part of Wigwas's persona.

Along the fence, Jasper shook his head as he was listening to Fast Ken tell him about Wigwas. Peter and Wigwas passed them. The rumour that carried out through the ballfield was that Peter tried to buy votes by promising to build people sheds. He owned part of a lumber company. Peter felt if Wigwas won the Best in the Rez, his new wife would feel comfortable around Wigwas and Wigwas would be the Great dog he is.

The white Pyrenees ran from Peter as they where about to walk in front of the judges. Wigwas wagged his tail and ran for the puddle. The puddle was as big as the Pyrenees and his fur soaked up all the water. Wigwas had a beautiful hunting motif beaded collar, beaded by the greatest beader in the Nation Sunshine. Peter commissioned the collar for the event. The collar was invisible. The mud covered everything. Peter walked toward Wigwas and pulled him from the puddle. Wigwas and Peter kept walking out the visitor's entrance.

❊❊❊

The first *Dog Show* was the only *Dog Show* ever on the Reserve. The Chief and the Doctor handed Juniper her winning trophy. The trophy was made from cedar and carved by the most beautiful man on the reserve, Handsome. Handsome carved a wolf/dog running with Best In Rez burned in below in a feathered banner.

Juniper and her brother Birch walked home with Seeker. They had popsicles and a bag of groceries. Their mother had just came home from work and they gave her the carved trophy. She put it on the mantle by the T.V. The remainder of the undisclosed winnings Birch and Juniper shared. It takes small wonders to make the Rez history files.

Seeker rested on top of their mother's car with a new soup bone.

THINGS WE BUILD

Matthew Heiti

Jeremy picks the bag of carrots off the counter and says, "These carrots are fucked."

I say, it's a big bag, five pounds and there's not a single good carrot in there?

He drops the bag like dirty laundry. "These carrots are fucked." The same thing he said yesterday when we got up, the same thing he said the day before and the day before that when he got here from the long drive and brought the frozen carrots up from the trunk of his car. The first piece of luggage out.

The phone rings.

I want Jeremy to tell me the metaphor here, the simile, whatever. Just tell me how this bag of carrots can be something that is going to hang all this mess together. They're not rotting, they don't smell or anything, they're not even bad. I mean, you can still eat them. They're just not that good anymore. They're not fresh and crunchy or vibrant orange. They sat in the back of your trunk from Portland to Sudbury and froze and then you brought them up here.

"You gonna answer your phone or what?"

I don't want to talk about the phone, I want to talk about carrots.

"They're fucked. I ate one. It was fucked."

I'm so hungry I feel sick, but I don't eat one because some friends you can trust and Jeremy's one of those friends.

Eventually, the phone stops ringing.

❋❋❋

Jeremy arrived on a Wednesday, leaves on a Monday. That's four whole days and two half days, so it's like a five day trip. Five days is a long time when you have three rooms to share and one of them is a bathroom.

Today is day four. We're hungover, him from alcohol, me from not sleeping, and I'm out of granola, so I get us out of the house and into his white Ford Tempo held together by rust and Saran wrap.

We perambulate the Scoop & Save, up and down the aisles full of bins. Jeremy asks me why I open this bin and that bin and smell, and I tell him it's because I'm checking how fresh they are. Not telling him I'm trying to live off aromas because my stomach is too busy killing itself right now.

Jeremy eats a wasabi cashew and I grab his arm and hiss something under my breath about the signs that say 'don't eat.' He pops a wasabi peanut in his mouth and turns the corner. What a little shit.

***

Standing at the counter of the bulk food store with two bills in my hand, thinking I can't spend this money. Don't need these soba noodles, these wasabi peas, this baggie of granola. The cashier staring at me, me staring at the Scoop & Save sign. Underneath that perky font, those two thick lines. One pink, one blue. Pink. Blue.

I can't spend this money, but I do because when you have company over and all they bring is carrots, carrots they refuse to eat, you have to feed them.

***

Jeremy stops at the beer store. We stare at the wall of beer logos in silence for twenty minutes before he gets rhetorical with, "They have anything good?"

We leave with a six of something auburn because that's different enough from pale or red for him to not make a face while he's drinking it. The six because tonight he's drinking alone, again.

Some people drink and some people don't. I usually do, sometimes quite a lot, but not right now. Right now, I'm a don't. And a won't. And an isn't. Right now, I'm not much of anything. Right now has been going on a long time. When you meet old friends, they often ask you what you're doing now. At my age, most people are done with jobs, they have careers and their five-year plans have become retirement packages. When people ask me what I'm doing I know they don't really care, it's just something you ask, so I usually say, not much. Not much is vague enough that I might be up to something important I don't feel like sharing or so esoteric they might not understand. I used to say I was hibernating because that's something you can wake up from.

❋❋❋

There's an envelope in the mailbox. No stamp, so she dropped it off. I stick it in my pocket before Jeremy can see and open the door. I can hear the phone ringing from the bottom of the stairs, but it's dead again before we push through into the stale air of my three rooms. I give Jeremy the bag of wasabi peas and a warm beer, the rest in the freezer because I know the pace of his drinking. I put my change in a tin can, because I should be trying to save. Then I open the cupboards, pull out a few cans, find a potato, get to cooking.

Jeremy sits on the kitchen floor, sipping his beer. He pulls off his tuque and rubs his head. Jeremy has short hair, like buzz-cut short. This is important because I wrote this other story in which he had long hair, like ponytail long. I never mentioned it there, but it's important because he pulls off his tuque and rubs his hair a lot, like he's remembering his ponytail. It's given him a new sadness, to add to his collection. Anyway, he still wears a tuque, even though it's spring. Some things never change.

This time when the phone starts ringing I cut myself chopping potatoes and Jeremy says "Dude. Your phone's ringing." Looks at me with those hangdog eyes, every joke buoyed by his misery. Waits a few more rings and then again with "Your phone's ringing."

Me watching the blood drip on the cutting board, the wood lapping it up.

❋❋❋

On the couch, he eats his soup. Four days ago I didn't have a couch and I told Jeremy he couldn't come visit until I got one. It arrived and then he arrived. Some things just work out I guess.

So far he hasn't asked anything about my not eating or not drinking, or not answering the phone. He hasn't asked much of anything. He either respects my privacy or he's too invested in his own tragedy. Mostly, he talks about his carrots.

❋❋❋

Something a.m. and I'm lying on my back thinking about my father. Thirty years of nine to five, five a week, two weeks a year, salary, benefits, pension, hating it all every second. Hating it so much to bring it home to sit at the dinner table with a place set for all that hate, spilling out with the plum sauce over chicken fingers. I work my ass off all day for fucking chicken fingers.

Thinking, Dad, you have a beard and I have a beard, but do I have to be like you?

I hold the envelope up in the light, paper glowing honey, something dark and waiting in the centre.

✳✳✳

You know how in stories or movies people always have these dreams that tie it all together? Like they have this dream that just sums up the theme or the message of the movie, but it's all weighed down with metaphors and crap so you have to crack the metaphor to get it. Like really get it. Well, if this were a movie, some independent Canadian movie you'd never see in a busted squeaky spring theatre in a burned out neighbourhood, I'd pass out at this point and have some dream.

I'd be a giant man-sized carrot, with arms and legs and my hair all green and tufted at the top. I'd be off and running down a long pink highway. I'd be alone and on my right side another highway, a blue one, would be fading in, and there would be another carrot running on that one. Day and night. This carrot would be all droopy, his green tuft hanging down like Jeremy's hangdog eyes, bits of carrot peeling off in the breeze, but no matter how fast I ran, he'd keep up. The blue of that highway coming in stronger with every step. Those two lines, blue and pink, stretching off into the horizon, never meeting. Underneath it all would be some jangly acid-jazz with a French chanteuse chanting "These carrots are fucked. These. Carrots. Are. Fucked."

After the film, you'd end up at some coffee shop talking the night away with your friends, everyone trying to be intellectual about what it all meant. Somebody saw most of a David Lynch movie this one time and he's a genius. And he gets it. Really gets it. He explains it to everybody and you all nod like you really get it too and then you all go home and sleep and have normal dreams that people don't have in movies.

But I don't sleep at all tonight. The only dreams I have are the ones you leave behind. At some point you have to make room for all that seriousness.

There's no room in here. Three rooms are not big enough.

✳✳✳

When I get up, Jeremy's at the kitchen counter poking at the bag of carrots, "These carrots are fucked." And it's day five of the carrots being fucked. Tomorrow Jeremy leaves and I can't wait, because I can get back to not doing all the things I need to do.

Jeremy drops in on me like this every now and then. It's impossible to predict, like a weather report he can give a forecast a few months in advance and then he just blows on in any old time. What can I tell you about him? Jeremy cooks for tree planters out west for four months every year. The rest of the time he drives around, his car collecting rust, him collecting calluses from all the couches he sleeps on.

When he's here he's like my little brother. Like all family he's under my skin in seconds and I'm frothing at the mouth. Five minutes later I love the guy.

Jeremy lives on the edge. What he's on the edge of I don't know, but it means he's usually broke and has no plans for the next day. What it does leave room for is spontaneity. You wake up and he's knocking and then tomorrow he vanishes, off on some adventure. Picking pinecones in Oregon. Some people say you shouldn't have regrets, or you can't be in the 'now.' I collect regrets. I like to have a lot of them. I like to trail one foot in the past like the dying drag one in the grave.

When Jeremy leaves tomorrow, I'll miss him because that's what you do when good people are gone.

✳✳✳

I'm in the shower and I can hear it ring in the other room. I could say it starts ringing but it's never really stopped, not in my brain, it just keeps going and going.

Then there's a chirp of it being cut off mid-ring and I know that little shit's answered the damn thing. I'm out sliding across wet tile, me ready with some tirade about unwritten rules, him sitting all quiet on the couch, phone on the coffee table in front of him.

"She wants you to call her."

He doesn't say anything about the absence of my towel. Some ironic comment on my nakedness. You have to believe in things to believe in irony and Jeremy doesn't believe in anything.

And now he knows.

✸✸✸

What can a friend do for you in a crisis? Offer a shoulder, a hand? Some sage advice? A kick in the ass? If you tell me what to do, I'll do it. Just tell me. But he can't. Jeremy doesn't offer me anything, and it's not because of that chicken soup sentiment you-can-only-help-those-blah-blah. He doesn't offer because he knows people can't help each other.

What he does is walk down the hill with me. This scene would be great in the rain, because it would be more ominous, me and Jeremy under the thunderclouds, but there's only sun up there. Kids out laughing in the streets, chasing the snowbank water running down gutters.

We push into the low brownstone library. Up and down aisles full of books, fluorescents buzzing on. I pull books out and I put books back. I decide on four, because five would look like too much, five would ooze desperation. Four I can get away with.

I practice a line about research, I'm writing a paper, but when I put them down the little librarian knows with a little smile. She knows and Jeremy knows. And there's so much more knowing in this room than I have inside me. They both know I'm going to be something and I'm so not this thing right now. This black sick space between those two swallowing me up. Out the doors, the books left on the counter.

✸✸✸

Jeremy pokes his head into room number two and throws the books at me, one at a time. He had to open his own account and he says I better return the books. I say it's not like you'll ever be back, and he says, I'm serious. I say, you can trust me.

"I know. So can you."

And he says it all light and walks out, like it might not mean anything at all.

And I know he can't let this sit because I might mistake it for sentiment. So he's back in ten minutes with a coat hanger and a jug of bleach, asking for her address. I say, that's not funny and he says, of course it is. I say, it's not about that and he says, about being funny, and I say no, about that. Jeremy doesn't get that this hasn't been a question, not even at the start. Pink and blue and we're on that highway and I'm not ready but it doesn't matter if I'm ready because it's coming and I can feel ring ring ring, tick tick tick, pat pat pat the carrot running down those twin highways, pink/blue, a steady rhythm of the coming. Jeremy, I squeeze out between laughs, Jeremy, I'm not ready. I'm not ready. Not ready to be something for someone smaller. Not ready to make room for all that love. I don't have enough. Three rooms is all I have and it's not enough.

And I don't want Jeremy to go in the morning. I don't want him to go because then he's gone and we're all moving forward and I can't stop him from leaving and I can't stop this. I'm laughing because I can't cry yet, it's not the end, it's the beginning and only endings make me cry. So all he can do is put down the coat hanger and pat me on the back, trying to comfort me while I laugh my guts out all over the place.

After he's gone to bed, I try to delete her messages. Hit the three twice and then seven, but I mess it up on the last one, just skipping forward instead of over, catching her last words, "It's growing toenails."

And it's not something big and loaded with symbolism like a heart or a brain that gets me. It's the thought of those little pink going cream slivers, looking down at my own big banged up toes on the hardwood floor. All the years of these feet on the ground walking and searching, and those ten little toenails all wrapped up and hidden, waiting to be seen.

❊❊❊

I'm not going to tell you all about her. Some people you can't do justice. I can tell you she's perfect, and not in some idealized way that fades when all the moony-eyed romance is gone. I mean she's perfect, for me. I knew it when we walked out of the rain into a bookstore and she said, we're going to find some Brautigan here. And we did. A whole shelf of first editions. But I only bought the ones she didn't have. Already picturing our collections falling together.

And if I'm going to be honest, guess I knew it when she shook my hand and said nice to meet you. People always say, you just know when you know. I used to roll my eyes. Now I know.

So it's never been a question because she just fits.

✳✳✳

I open the envelope. Expecting confusion, expecting disappointment, expecting rage. Finding expecting. Four little strips. Eight little stripes. Pink, blue. A chorus. And a note, the water flow of her handwriting, 'for the scrapbook.'

✳✳✳

Jeremy's left a book that I didn't pick out. It's some home reno book called *Things We Build*. On the cover's this cheap little cartoon of a husband and wife in overalls and behind them their house is in ruins. The roof's caving in, flames leaping out of the second story and there they are with their arms around each other looking all overjoyed. And something about this stupid cartoon reminds me of how we built my bed frame. Without fighting. Her working on one side, passing me the tools when I needed them, taking them back when she needed them, this thing growing around us as we worked.

✳✳✳

And then there was that old photo album we bought in a junk shop. The sign said 'Antiques' but I didn't see any. And we started to use it as a scrapbook. I know, you think 'ever cute,' like we're going to put photos of us being happy all over the place. But neither of us even owns a camera. So we put things like the receipt from the first sandwich she brought me, or a maple key I found while we were having a good walk, the first condom wrapper. But it's not just the cutesy stuff. There's a cigarette butt from the night we had our first fight. A bus ticket from the trip down to her brother's funeral.

All falling together between the pages because that's a life. Ours anyway. And it's all worth keeping somewhere.

Now four little tests. Positive, positive, positive, positive. Ten little toenails. And I've never been so sure.

I'm going to call her and then I'm not going to call her and then I pick up the phone but there's no dial tone and I know I'm caught in one of the rare moments where you answering and her calling just sort of bleed into one another. I don't say anything, she doesn't say anything and the silence sits heavy. Not like we don't know what to say but that there's something too large for words going on. She doesn't say something's wrong and I don't say I'm on my way, but we know these things when we don't say them.

I run all the way, forever of running and I'm not the best in-shape guy I know, but I'm not even breathing hard when I get there.

This is me at the bottom of her stairs.

I'm not going to tell you what happens when I get up there. I'm not going to say she's in the bathroom crying and it's all gone red in the toilet. I'm not going to tell you that I told her, it's alright, we can put that red in the collection with the four positive tests, that this will still be our story. That I love this red like I really did love those little toenails, like I'll really love all the things we build.

I'm not going to tell you all that because it's poetry and it's bullshit and nothing ever ties together like that. You never find the perfect words at the right moment. I'm not going to tell you anything because it would take all this breath I've been holding inside for so long, and I need it to climb these stairs. To go in.

✳✳✳

I can tell you that I get rained on all the way home and when I get there Jeremy and his Ford Tempo are gone. But not the bag of carrots. The birds are going on out there in the rain, first morning of the birds, that rain coming down hard, but not ominous the way I pictured it. There's a wet smell in the kitchen and I know the carrots are starting to rot. But this isn't a movie and so the carrot thing isn't about me. It really isn't. I'm not rotting or anything. I cry right there on my kitchen floor because it's the ending. But it's not really, because it's the first morning of the birds and the rain is coming down so hard and fast that everything will be clean soon. And here comes the spring growing around me.

AUTHOR BIOS

Rosanna Micelotta Battigelli

Rosanna was born in Italy and immigrated to Canada with her family when she was three. She developed a love for language and reading early in life and majored in Italian and French at Laurentian University. She has taught Kindergarten to Grade 8 with the Sudbury Catholic District School Board, and was awarded four Best Practice Awards from the Ontario English Catholic Teacher's Association. Rosanna has been published in Canadian anthologies, and has received mentoring at the Humber School for Writers. While writing her recently-completed historical novel, Rosanna received an Ontario Arts Council Writer's Works in Progress Grant.

Lara Bradley

Lara is a Sudbury writer who writes flash fiction stories and sometimes plays, including Blind Nickel Pig, Sperm Wars, and is one of four collaborators of the commissioned play #WaterTower for the Sudbury Theater Centre. The Dust of My Own Moon started as a sliver of a story for The Flanneurs writing group (Matt Heiti and Kristina Donato) and was inspired by the song Silverado. A former Sudbury Star reporter, she still does some freelance work, although her day job is in communications. Lara loves spending time outdoors with her teenage sons, Sebastian and Quinn, and husband Peter Zwarich.

Rob Dominelli

Robert is a life-long Sudbury resident and a father of four. Always keen on the written word, Robert enjoyed writing as a youth but gave it up, believing it would never amount to anything. He spent much of the late nineties in a cycle of dependency and incarceration. During his last stint in jail he began writing again, silly little offensive stories to amuse other inmates. Robert continued writing fiction after his release. Writing gives Robert a sense of self-worth, and a clear path to a future free of concrete and cast iron.

Kim Fahner

Kim lives and writes in Sudbury, Ontario, teaching English at
Marymount Academy. She has published three books of poetry, *You
Must Imagine The Cold Here* (Scrivener Press, 1997), *Braille on Water*
(Penumbra Press, 2001), and *The Narcoleptic Madonna* (Penumbra
Press, 2012). In the late 1990s, she worked with Timothy Findley as her
mentor via the Humber School for Writers program. In Spring 2013,
she took part in The Battle of the Bards at Toronto's Harbourfront. In
July 2014, she attended The Sage Hill Writing Experience in Lumsden,
Saskatchewan, working with Ken Babstock as her mentor. She is
a member of the League of Canadian Poets, the Writers Union of
Canada, and PEN Canada. Kim is currently finishing her fourth book
of poetry, working on her first novel, and has just finished her first play,
which will be performed at the Sudbury Theatre Centre in the coming
season. You can read her non-fiction blog posts on "The Republic of
Poetry" at kimfahner.wordpress.com.

Matthew Heiti

Matthew holds an MA in Creative Writing from the University of New
Brunswick. His writing has appeared in many of his favourite journals
and his first novel, *The City Still Breathing*, is published by Coach House
Books. He was named one of CBC's "Writers to Watch" in 2014. His
plays have been workshopped and produced at theatres and festivals
across Canada. He is a Genie-nominated screenwriter and his play
for teens, *Black Dog: 4 vs. The World,* will be published by Playwrights
Canada Press in 2016. In his spare time, he is usually working. Some of
his writing can be found at: www.harkback.org.

Liisa Kovala

Liisa is a Finnish-Canadian teacher and writer living in Sudbury,
Ontario with her husband and two children. She is a member of the
Canadian Authors Association and Sudbury Writers' Guild. Her fiction
and non-fiction pieces have appeared in Chicken Soup for the Soul:
Christmas in Canada, CommuterLit.com, Sudbury Living, Canadian

Stories and Canadian Teacher Magazine. Her family memoir *A Day Soon Dawns* was self-published in March 2015. Liisa's work explores her Finnish heritage and northern community.

Thomas Leduc

Thomas lives and works in Sudbury. He has been writing poetry for several years and is the current Poet Laureate of the City of Greater Sudbury and a member of the Sudbury Writers' Guild. In 2012, Thomas won a poetry contest put on by the Vale Living with Lakes Centre for his poem *My Northern Lake*. It was published in the *Our Lakes Shall Set Us Free* anthology and hangs above the Margaret Atwood fireplace in the Living with Lakes Centre in Sudbury. Tom has had poems published in issues 3 and 5 of Laurentian University's Literary Journal, *Sulphur*.

Karen McCauley

Karen is an Assistant Professor at Laurentian University's School of Social Work and a life-long resident of the Sudbury region. She collects stories and writes recreationally, often as a liberating diversion from the sometimes constraining demands of academic research and writing. Increasingly, however, she finds herself returning to fiction to inform and illustrate that research. As someone who looks forward to going back to school in the fall, writing *At the Gas Station* was an opportunity to look back over familiar landscapes.

Eric Moore

Over the course of his working life Eric Moore has been employed as a janitor, shipping receiver, security guard, handy man, and radio announcer/host. He began writing short stories and poetry in the early 1990's. Several of his stories have won prizes in literary competitions. His poems have been published in various anthologies including *Arc Poetry Magazine* and *Oval Victory*. Eric lives with his wife and two cats in the wilds of New Sudbury.

Darlene Naponse

Darlene is an Anishinaabe from Atikameksheng Anishnawbek – Northern Ontario, where she was born and raised. She is a writer, film director, video artist and community activist. Her film work has been viewed internationally including the Sundance Film Festival in 2001, '02, '03. Her film *Every Emotion Costs* screened worldwide, winning various awards. Her art based video work has been installed in various galleries and programs nationally/internationally. She is currently working on a book of short stories. She owns Pine Needle Productions an award-winning boutique Film/Audio Recording Production Studio, located in Atikameksheng Anishnawbek. Darlene is passionate and pure as an independent artist.

Tina Siegel

Tina is a Sudbury girl living in Toronto (until she can make her way back home). She writes poetry and short stories inspired by bits and pieces of real life and embellished by her imagination. She has participated in writing workshops with Shaughnessy Bishop-Stall, and recently completed Humber College's online Creative Writing program with Camilla Gibb. When she's not writing, she's teaching English, teasing her cat, or playing with the dogs that live in her apartment building.

Casey Stranges

Casey is a freelance copywriter based in Sudbury, Ontario. He was the consulting editor for *Sulphur: Laurentian University's Literary Journal* and continues to assist Laurentian students in the fields of journalism and communications. Casey's work has appeared in local news and trade publications for the underground mining and corporate security industries, as well as public relations work for small not-for-profit organizations in the Sudbury area. His first published work of fiction appeared in *The Other Gender*, an anthology of University of Toronto writers.

Laura E. Young

Laura is a Sudbury-based journalist and the author of *Solo Yet Never Alone Swimming the Great Lakes*, the story of the mindset it takes to swim Earth's largest reservoir of fresh water. She's currently working on her second book. During her career in journalism and communications, Laura has written about everything from astroparticle physics to zoology. She writes *The Sudbury Star*'s Personal Best sports column and is renowned for her coverage of amateur and community-based sport. First and foremost, Laura is a swimmer; Water's supreme value is a theme flowing through all her work.

Editor

Mitchell Gauvin is a Toronto-born, Sudbury-raised writer and editor who has also spent time in Montreal and Dublin. His short stories and poetry have appeared in a variety of publications including *NEST by Gutterbird*, *The Varsity*, *CanCulture*, and *Feathertale*. His debut novel, *Vandal Confession*, was released in Fall 2015. He is a graduate of the University of Toronto and University College Dublin.

Cover Artist

Danielle Daniel writes and paints stories. She is a mixed-media artist inspired by her Métis roots. Her artwork is sold internationally and has been widely published. In 2015, Groundwood Books published her children's book *Sometimes I Feel Like a Fox*. Danielle's short stories have been published in Room and forthcoming in Event Magazine. She is currently enrolled in the MFA program in Creative Writing at the University of British Columbia where she is busy at work on a novel. She lives in Greater Sudbury, with her husband Steve, son Owen and their dogs Frodo and Suzie.